"I got no need of a man."

"I ain't offering to marry you."

Lucy snorted. "That's not exactly what I meant. I meant to escort me to the recitation."

Wade refused to repent. "I still ain't offering." He had been alone for a long time. Preferred it that way.

They reached the schoolroom. Lucy led him to a desk near the front and they crowded in side by side. He noted how nicely she fit next to him.

Again he marveled that a body as pretty and as sweet smelling as Lucy's—like a field of clover in full bloom—could house a heart of coal.

Thankfully it was time for the program to begin. He forced his attention back to the front of the room. Then Lucy rose.

For a moment, he couldn't take his eyes off her, then he forced himself to remember why he was here.

Lucy—with her grey eyes and teasing smile—had succeeded in throwing open all the gates in his thoughts. But he wasn't here to moon over a gal. He cared only for one thing—convincing Lucy to visit her father.

Books by Linda Ford

Love Inspired Historical

The Road to Love
The Journey Home
The Path to Her Heart
Dakota Child
The Cowboy's Baby
Dakota Cowboy

LINDA FORD

shares her life with her rancher husband, a grown son, a live-in client she provides care for and a yappy parrot. She and her husband raised a family of fourteen children, ten adopted, providing her with plenty of opportunity to experience God's love and faithfulness. They had their share of adventures, as well. Taking twelve kids in a motorhome on a three-thousand-mile road trip would be high on the list. They live in Alberta, Canada, close enough to the Rockies to admire them every day. She enjoys writing stories that reveal God's wondrous love through the lives of her characters.

Linda enjoys hearing from readers. Contact her at linda@lindaford.org or check out her Web site at www.lindaford.org, where you can also catch her blog, which often carries glimpses of both her writing activities and family life.

Dakota Cowboy

LINDA FORD

Steeple
Hill®

Published by Steeple Hill Books™

STEEPLE HILL BOOKS

Steeple
Hill®

Recycling programs
for this product may
not exist in your area.

ISBN-13: 978-0-373-82839-5

DAKOTA COWBOY

www.SteepleHill.com

Printed in U.S.A.

In thy presence is fullness of joy; at thy right hand there are pleasures for evermore.

—*Psalms* 16:11

To God be the glory. As Jesus said in *John* 15:5, "Apart from me you can do nothing." I am aware of my limitations every day and grateful for His sufficiency.

Chapter One

Summer 1896, Dry Creek, North Dakota

He looked like any one of the hundred different cowboys who came in pretending they wanted a nice meal in a fancy dining room when what they really wanted was to eyeball the girl serving the food.

Yes, he looked like every other cowboy except for his steady eyes and how quiet and still he held himself, all watchful and calm.

Eighteen-year-old Lucy Hall served dozens of men like him every day—ignoring their invitations to walk her home, smiling at their jokes, ducking away from those who would steal a touch. None of them made her look twice.

Until now.

It was the way he seemed so self-assured, so peaceful with himself that drew her glance to him time after time. Often she caught a little smile on his lips as he overheard something from a nearby table. She wished she could share his amusement, grab hold a bit of his calmness. He gave her the feeling all was right with his world.

Lucy hesitated just a fraction on her way to get his order. No one would have noticed the slight pause if they'd cared to glance up from their meal. Only she knew the way her heart skittered with something akin to the nervousness she'd felt the first day she'd worked in the Dry Creek Hotel dining room.

"Morning, sir, what can I get you?" The words caught on the back of her tongue, but she would not clear her throat and cause any of the patrons to glance her way nor give them reason to tease her.

He smiled. His eyes were blue-green, like pond water on a bright day. He owned an unruly mop of blond curls.

Her cheeks heated as if seared by a July sun.

"You here alone?"

The sunshine threatened to blind her, though she knew the curtains muted the morning light. Her feeling of being shone upon had come from his smile, his eyes. She pulled her thoughts into orderly control and turned her concentration to his question. Was the man joshing? No, she sadly mused. Only like a hundred other cowboys wanting to sweet-talk her. She knew how to handle them. Tease them. Pretend to play along with their nonsense while guarding her words, her thoughts and her emotions. "Let's see. Apart from—" she glanced around the room "—about a dozen others and Harry and Hettie in the kitchen, yup, I'm pretty much alone."

He tipped his head back and laughed. "Guess that was a stupid question. It's just that I was told—I wondered if there was another girl helping you."

Lucy's nerves danced in accompaniment to his chuckle. She sniffed in air heavy with the smell of bacon and fried potatoes. He was like a hundred others she saw every day.

Only he wasn't. She wished she could put her finger on what made him different—besides the fact he made her nervous and excited all at once.

"I'll have a good-sized breakfast, please and thank you."

Please and thank you. Well, that was different. "Eggs? Sausage? Bacon? Steak? Hash browns?"

"Yup. The works, if you don't mind. I'm feeling just a mite hungry."

She chuckled. "Better bring a pocket full of bills if you ever develop a big hunger."

He favored her with another white-toothed smile. That was different, too. Most cowboys neglected their teeth, allowing the tobacco so many chewed to discolor them in a most atrocious way. "And coffee, please."

Lucy left the table, walked over to the pass-through window and called, "Starving Bachelor's Special."

Hettie snorted. "Pile it high?"

"Man says he's a mite hungry."

"Gotcha."

Lucy reached for a fine-china teacup and saucer. She loved the way so many of the men sputtered when she handed them the dainty things. She'd chuckle and leave them struggling to figure out how to hold the tiny handle. She filled the cup with scalding coffee and took it to the cowboy who picked it up with perfect calmness. Yes, that was different, too. This man was beginning to interest her. Who was he and what was he doing in the Dry Creek dining room?

She refilled a few more customers coffee cups before returning the coffeepot to the stove.

"Bachelor breakfast ready." Hettie wiped her sweaty brow on her wide, white apron.

Lucy grabbed the waiting plate of food and took it to the quiet cowboy.

He dropped his gaze to his plate. She could practically hear the rush of juice in his mouth. He held his fork and knife, poised as if ready to do battle with the teetering pile of food.

She sensed his reluctance to eat while she hovered at his side. "I'll bring more coffee."

"Much appreciated."

Still, she hesitated wanting…she knew not what.

But she had other things to attend to and she took the coffeepot and began to refill cups on other tables.

"Lucy gal, order up," Hettie called in her beefy voice.

"Oh, Lucy gal, you can order me up whenever you want."

Lucy filled the leering man's cup and ducked out of reach.

"Lucy gal, Lucy gal." A row of patrons—all male, all ranchers and rough cowboys—hoisted their cups and leaned over, begging for refills.

Lucy hurried down the line, dancing out of reach, laughing at their teasing. There was a time they had scared her, made her tense and anxious. She soon learned the best way to deal with them was to turn it into a game. That way they all had fun. And if anyone got rowdy or out of line, Harry, Hettie's husband and owner of the dining room, would hustle them out the door so fast they dug ruts in the polished wooden floor. Harry tolerated no unruly or rude behavior, and Harry was brawny enough that no one argued with his rules.

She took the coffeepot to the hungry cowboy and refilled his cup.

"*You're* Lucy?" he asked.

She tipped her head to one side and planted a finger in the middle of her chin. "Now, I can't imagine how you'd know that. Oh, unless it's because the name has been hooted, bandied about and generally abused for the last ten minutes."

He nodded, his eyes suddenly watchful, guarded

even. She couldn't think why he should look at her in such a way. But she didn't have time to wonder for long. Duty called and she got back to work.

After she'd been back to his table to refill his cup a fourth time she stifled a giggle as she glanced at his ears. It wouldn't surprise her none to see twin spouts of brown liquid gushing from each side of his head.

By now, only the coffee-swilling, no-longer-hungry cowboy and an older couple remained in the dining room. Lucy began to wonder if someone had smeared his chair with glue before he sat down. Wouldn't Harry have a conniption if they had?

His presence trickled along her nerves, making her very aware of him as she put fresh white cloths on each of the tables, and set out china and silverware in preparation for the customers who would come for the noon meal.

Harry charged into the room and glanced around. He took note of the lone cowboy before he poured himself a cup of coffee and sat down to read some papers.

He glanced again at the cowboy and slid Lucy an inquiring look. She read his silent message. *Is this fella bothering you?*

She shrugged. How did she explain the way she felt drawn to him? Hoping…for what? That he'd hung about waiting for a chance to speak to her? Lots of the patrons waited for such a chance. If he had something to say, best he come right out and say it.

Not one to play coy games, she grabbed the coffee-pot and headed in his direction. He was no different than any of the other cowboys who came and went. Most of them she didn't give a passing glance. A few she favored with a walk out, or accompanied to a play or some activity put on by the cultural society. If this one asked, would she agree to go? Yes, she would because there *was* something different about him. She couldn't put her finger on it. She only knew there was something in the way he *didn't* look at her. His stare was not openly curious and measuring like so many of the cowboys—as if they were checking her for conformity, estimating her hardiness—judging her like she a good beef animal.

"Another refill?"

He pushed away his cup. "No, thank you, ma'am. Mighty fine it was, though." He edged his chair back and looked at her, a hard glint in his eyes.

Lucy hesitated. What had happened to change the softer, kinder look she'd first noticed? But what did it matter? He was only one of hundreds of cowboys she served.

Wade Miller struggled to get his mind around the discovery that this was Lucy Hall—Scout's daughter. At first glance, he had been mesmerized by her bubbly personality that had every pair of eyes in the full dining room following her with amused appreciation. Who would know from the way she acted that beneath the surface lay a heart as cold as river ice? What kind of girl would return her father's letters unread and refuse continued invitations to visit?

He was here to change that.

She hovered at his side with the bottomless coffeepot. He planted his hand firmly over the top of his mug. His eyeballs were already drowning.

"I'm done. Thank you very much."

She nodded and told him the total for his breakfast.

He made to pull the money from his pocket and paused. Slowly, cautiously, he brought his gaze to her. She wore the same amused expression he'd observed throughout the morning.

"Something I can do for you, mister?"

He didn't like tipping his head to talk to her and pushed his chair back so he could gain his feet and full height. That was better. Now she had to tip her head, which set her pale brown hair to quivering. He'd once seen hair that color on an old dog he was particularly fond of. The animal had the smarts of a fox and the heart of a saint. For a dog the fur had been silky enough but he was willing to believe Lucy's hair was a whole lot silkier. And a thousand times sweeter smelling.

He jerked his thoughts back to reality. Nice hair did not change the cruelness of her heart.

"You're Lucy Hall, I take it."

"Where you plan to take it, mister?"

He grinned. She'd given him the perfect opening. "I'd like to take it and you to see your father."

She stepped back and curled her lips like he had a bad smell.

"My father sent you?"

Coming here had been his idea, not Scout's. "He figured you hadn't received his letters."

She planted her hands on her hips. "You tell him I got them just fine. You tell him I don't care to hear from him. You tell him—" She gasped in air like a horse that had been rode too long and too hard.

He wasn't about to give up just because some little filly was all tangled up in some sort of hornets nest. "He's sick. Wants to see you. Seems reasonable enough."

She leaned forward, her chin jutted out, her eyes warning of approaching thunder. "Mister, you had your say. I suggest you move on."

"Trouble, Lucy gal?" The big man Wade took to be the owner breathed down his neck. Every nerve in his body jerked to full alert. He knew better than to mess with a man that size and with that warning note in his voice.

"I'm on my way." But he'd be back.

He left the dining room and swung into the saddle. He rode past a rowdy bar. Knew the cowboys would be filling up the hotel rooms come nighttime. He could buy himself a bed but he was used to his own company. Preferred it to the sort he'd find crawling around town.

He reined his horse toward the thin stand of trees where he intended to set up camp. He unsaddled Two Bit and tossed him a handful of oats. He'd let him roam, picking what he could. The horse would come as soon as he whistled.

After finding a rock to lean his back on, Wade settled down to think. The heat beat at his skin. It caused the landscape to sway like grass in the wind. Nothing blocked his view of the town. A struggling prairie town with high hopes, few trees.

Nothing about this scenery compared to the ranch in the hills, to the west. There, grass grew high as a horse's belly, a house sat in the shade of cottonwoods, and a pretty little creek made a beautiful sound as it washed over rocks. No one could see the ranch without loving it. Not even someone like Lucy. He was equally certain that if she saw Scout she would forget whatever little tiff had made her shut him out of her life.

He could drive a herd of cows and rope a wild mustang but how did a cowboy persuade a reluctant, beautiful woman to go where she didn't want to go?

He intended to find a way. Maybe he could even use some help from God. He hadn't put much stock in the faith his mother had taught him until last winter, but there was no denying God had answered his desperate prayer back then. He wasn't sure if he had the right to ask anything more of the Man up above but figured it wouldn't hurt.

God, Scout looked about to die when I left. He hoped he could fulfill this task he had given himself before the man drew his last breath. *Seems only reasonable that he get the chance to see his daughter before he does. Might help if You show this Lucy gal that she should pay her father a visit.*

He returned to town a few hours later and passed some time nosing about. As the evening shadows lengthened, he thought of riding to the front door of the dining room and going in for supper, but Harry had been a little less than welcoming in his final goodbye. But having asked around, he knew Lucy would be done as soon as the supper crowd left. He'd not been able to discover where she lived. People tended to be a little suspicious if his questions were too direct.

He decided he'd wait at the back of the Dry Creek dining room and reined his horse in that direction. Sooner or later he'd get a chance to talk to her, persuade her to visit her father. Once she knew the precarious nature of Scout's health, there'd be no way she could refuse.

He slid from Two Bit's back, and let the horse lounge in the shade provided by the board fence at the side of the alley. He leaned back against the rough lumber and got himself comfortable, pulling his hat low to shade his eyes. Anyone seeing him might think he slept on his feet. They'd be wrong. His ears registered every skittering bit of dirt, every creak of the fence, every footfall.

He cracked one eye at the patter of running feet. A small ragamuffin of a boy skidded to a halt fifteen feet away and stared from Wade to Two Bit. He heard the boy's sharply indrawn breath, took note of his sudden wary stiffening and hid a smile as the youngster just as quickly donned a sullen expression and a slouch before he plucked a blade of grass from beside the fence, stuck it in his mouth and swaggered to the door of the dining room to lean back as bold and unconcerned as if he had his name on the deed.

Wade used one finger to tip his hat back. "Howdy."

"Howdy." The boy gave a barely there nod and a bold, uncompromising stare.

Wade lowered his hat again and settled back.

"You waiting for something?" For a youngster so scrawny Wade could practically count his ribs through his thin shirt, he sure did have a challenging way of talking.

"Just waiting."

"You hoping to see Lucy, ain't ya?"

"It concern you if I am?"

The boy scowled something fierce like a kid used

to fighting his way through life. "Lucy don't care for drifters hanging about."

"Can't say as I blame her."

The boy snorted.

Wade shoved his hat back and came off the fence so fast the boy flattened himself to the wall. "Name's Wade. Wade Miller." He shoved his hand toward the boy.

"Roy. Just Roy." He took Wade's outstretched hand. His grip surprisingly firm for such an under-nourished-looking body.

"Pleased to make your acquaintance, Roy." He leaned back, studying Roy. "You waiting for Lucy?" Did the boy have some claim on her? Too old to be her son. Maybe a brother, though Scout had never mentioned such.

"Just waiting."

Wade gave him a steady look. He didn't say it but he thought, *Kid, don't bother trying to whitewash the truth with me.*

Roy must have read the unspoken words in Wade's eyes. He rolled the end of the grass around in his mouth to inform Wade he might or might not choose to tell him more. "Lucy gives me a plate of food every night."

Wade ran his gaze over the scrawny kid. "Looks like you could do with a good feeding."

"Lucy says it's impossible to fill a growing boy."

"How old are you, Roy?"

"Ten. But I can do a man's work. I work over at the livery barn. Mr. Peterson gives me a place to sleep in exchange for cleaning the barn and seeing the horses have feed and water." The words came out in a rush as if Roy needed Wade to understand his value.

"Where's your ma and pa?"

Roy's expression grew indifferent. "Ain't got none."

A rattle at the doorknob pulled their attention to the Dry Creek dining room. Lucy stepped out with a plate piled halfway to the roof. "Hettie said there were lots of leftovers today. You'll get a good feed tonight." She ruffled Roy's hair and beamed at him. "I see you washed up."

Roy had his face buried in the food but spared her a pained look. "'Course I did. What you think I am? A...a...?" He couldn't seem to find a fitting word and tilted his head in Wade's direction instead. "Who's he?"

Lucy jerked back, finally realizing his presence. Her expression grew a whole lot less welcoming. "What are you doing here?"

Wade snatched off his hat. "Ma'am, I just want to talk to you."

"I think you already said all I want to hear."

"What's he want?" Roy spoke around a mouth crammed with food.

"Don't talk with your mouth full. He's nobody. Just another cowboy. I see hundreds of them."

Roy wisely ignored her comment and continued shoveling in food but his eyes darted from Lucy to Wade.

"All I ask is that you allow me to explain the whole thing." Once she knew how desperate the situation was, she'd surely agree to visit the ranch.

Roy paused from inhaling food. "You got no one to take you to the recitation tonight. He could take you."

At the look Lucy gave Roy, Wade wondered if the boy would have singe marks.

"I don't need an escort."

Roy shrugged. "You said you don't like walking home alone after dark."

"You must have misunderstood me."

Roy stopped chewing. He looked like she'd personally called him a liar. Like her approval of him meant more than the food itself. The boy scraped the last of the food into his mouth and ran his tongue over the plate. Well, maybe not more than food. But he was obviously hurt by Lucy's remark.

Lucy saw it, too. Her expression flicked toward regret. "I'll be fine, Roy. Don't you worry about me."

Wade saw his chances of Lucy agreeing to accompany him slipping away. "This here recitation—it's like a meeting thing?"

"Lucy has a poem to say." Roy sounded as proud as a papa.

"It's the literary society." Lucy's tone made it plain that a cowboy wouldn't enjoy such.

"I like recitations." A lifetime ago he'd hovered behind a half-closed door and listened to recitations and music playing in the drawing room of the house where his ma worked. "I'd like to go if it's open to cowboys."

She didn't miss his mocking tone and looked slightly regretful.

"Go with him," Roy urged. "Ain't you the one to always say a person shouldn't be afraid to take a chance now and then?"

Lucy closed her eyes and sighed deeply. "Roy, do you write down everything I say and commit it to memory to quote at the most awkward moments?"

Roy got that hurt look again but Lucy smiled at him and squeezed his shoulder.

"You'll go?"

"Of course I'll go. I'm going to recite."

Roy shook his head. "I mean with him."

Lucy studied Roy a long moment. "I don't see why it's so important to you."

"I want you to be safe."

Lucy ruffled his hair. "For you, I'll do it." She faced Wade, an expression of pure stubbornness on her face. "On one condition." She waited for him to accept.

"Can't hardly agree to something when I don't know what it is."

"You promise not to talk about my father."

He swallowed, weighing his options. His primary reason for wanting to go to the event had been to explain why Lucy must visit her father. But a pack of other reasons overtook that one. It had been a lifetime or two since he'd heard poetry. He imagined Lucy speaking with the laughter in her voice that she seemed to reserve for everyone but him. But poetry and a musical voice mattered not. He had to convince Lucy to visit her father. Perhaps if he bided his time, she would get curious and ask after Scout.

"Deal." Yes, he'd promised not to talk about her father. He hadn't, however, promised not to talk about himself.

Chapter Two

Wade couldn't help but stare at Lucy. When he'd first seen her, serving in the dining room, she'd worn a black skirt, a white top and a crisp white apron with frills along the edges. Her hair had been up in a tight bun although bits of it had come loose. She now wore a dark pink dress with a wide pink ribbon around her tiny waist. A few more strands of hair had also fallen loose from her bun. She looked very pretty. Like some kind of candy.

Wade glanced down at his trousers, suddenly aware he might not be fit to attend a literary society function. But having gained Lucy's agreement to let him accompany her, he wasn't about to let his lack of Sunday-go-to-meeting clothes hinder him.

She tilted her head in the direction they were to go.

He whistled for Two Bit to follow, nodded goodbye to Roy and fell in at Lucy's side.

She waited until they turned from the alley into the street before she spoke. "I'm only doing this for Roy."

Her words were so unnecessary he couldn't help but laugh. "And all this time I thought it was my irresistible charm. You sure do know how to cut a man down to size."

She looked vaguely troubled by his comment. "I got no need of a man."

"I ain't offering to marry you."

"That's not what I meant. I meant I don't need a man to escort me to the recitation."

"I still ain't offering." He had been alone for a long time. Preferred it that way.

They reached the schoolroom that apparently served as home to the literary society and crowded inside with the others. All the windows had been shoved up and the doors at both ends propped open to let in air. Still, the place was like an oven ready for baking bread. Lucy led him to a desk near the front and they crowded in side by side. It was a tight squeeze. He noted how nicely she fit at his side, her head inches above his shoulder so every time he turned her way he could study how straight and fine her nose was. He could admire the color of her hair again and see how it shone in the slanting light from the open door. He squeezed his hands together to keep from touching her hair, aching to know if it felt as silky as it looked. He realized he still wore his hat and snatched it off to scrunch it to his lap.

Again he marveled that a body as pretty and as sweet-smelling as Lucy's—like a field of clover in full bloom—could house a heart of coal. He tightened his mouth. He'd endure her pressed to his side, tolerate how nice she smelled and ignore the way her hair begged to be touched all for the sake of finding a chance to persuade her to show some human decency and visit her father.

Thankfully, it was soon time for the program to begin and he could concentrate on the proceedings.

A man with a handlebar moustache stood and welcomed everyone. And then the recitations began. Wade laughed at the story of a man searching for his horse and running into all sorts of calamities. His amusement grew by leaps and bounds as he met Lucy's laughing eyes. He forced his attention back to the front of the room as a frail lady recited two Psalms. A young girl did a sweet poem of hope and love. Then Lucy rose. She fairly glowed as she began to speak, putting her heart into every word.

Wade had heard the poem before and knew what to expect, but enjoyed it just as much as the others who alternated between laughter and tears.

Lucy returned to her place at his side amidst clapping, cheering and shouts of "Bully for you, Lucy gal." Twin roses bloomed on her cheeks. She gave Wade a look he could only interpret as triumphant.

For a moment, he couldn't take his eyes off her then he forced himself to remember why he was here and what she was like beneath all that charm and good humor.

Three more recitations and the program ended. Wade bolted to his feet, his chest tight with a nameless anxiety. He had to get Lucy alone so he could talk to her, explain why it was so necessary to make the trek to the ranch.

But before his muddled brain could devise a plan, a black-clad woman called for their attention. "Tea and cake will be served outside. Ten cents each. Remember the money all goes to buying a bell for our church."

"Let's go." Lucy grabbed his arm. "I want to get a piece of Mrs. Adam's chocolate cake."

Seemed everyone had the same idea. A stampede tried to squeeze out the door, pushing Lucy tight to Wade's side. He discovered she not only fit like they were meant for each other, but that it was going to be nearly impossible to keep his thoughts on the purpose of his visit. He grunted as someone elbowed him. "Trouble with being at the front is you're the tail going out," he murmured.

Lucy groaned. "I know all that chocolate cake will be gone."

A young man in a suit and tie, with a complexion the color of biscuit dough, allowed himself to be jostled against Lucy. Wade felt her stiffen, knew she didn't appreciate the boldness of this dandified man. Wade edged forward just enough to push the man away. And then they were through the door, in the open where a person could breathe without inhaling someone else's air. He grabbed Lucy's elbow and hustled her to the table. 'Course he didn't have to do much hustling. He was hard-pressed to keep up to her as she made the hundred-yard dash to the table covered with a selection of cakes. He dropped twenty cents into the plate and got two cups of tea in exchange.

"Look, there's a piece left." She dived for it and emerged crowing with triumph. A thought seemed to choke her pleasure. She glanced from the cake to Wade. Doubt clouded her face. "I could…"

She was considering giving up her cake after wrestling it from the kid behind her who now glared daggers at her. "You'd never forgive me." He did not need her to hold a grudge over some cake. And to prove his point, he scooped up a large piece of spice cake with brown sugar icing, followed her away from the table to one of the benches and sat down.

Lucy ate the cake like it was a matter of life and death. She licked her fingers. Barely resisted licking the plate. He was so fascinated with her enthusiasm he forgot to test his own piece of cake.

She must have seen the wonder in his expression. "You have no idea how delicious it is."

"Was."

She eyed her plate.

"You ate the whole thing."

"I offered it to you."

"Yup." He took a bite of his own selection. "This ain't half bad either."

"Like comparing beans and peaches. Both good but—" She shrugged, letting him know he got the beans but she wasn't a bit regretful.

He mused about how best to bring up the topic of the ranch without mentioning her father. "I heard that poem before. My ma used to work in a house where they had literary gatherings. She loved that poem. Guess that's why I like it."

"You mean the poem I recited?" She grinned. "Or the one about chasing the horse?"

Far as he was concerned, only one poem stood out as being worthy of mention. "Yours. It made me miss her."

"Where is she?"

"Died some years ago."

"I'm sorry. My ma is dead, too."

Another thing Scout neglected to tell him. "I guess you never stop missing your ma." Though he'd started missing his ma long before she died. Once she started working for the Collins family after Pa's untimely death, she'd never had time for him.

Lucy nodded. "I don't expect I'll ever forget my ma or the lessons I learned from her."

He wanted to talk to her, ask her about her mother,

tell her about the ranch but a continual string of people came by to say howdy-do to Lucy. She laughed and joked with them all. She had an easy way about her, as if life fit her well.

Someone came by and picked up the empty cups and plates.

Lucy sprang to her feet. "I could of done that. I'll help with the dishes."

The lady, the same black-garbed woman who had announced the refreshments, tittered and batted her eyes at Wade. "No, no, dear. You enjoy your beau."

"My beau?" Lucy sputtered so hard Wade whacked her between the shoulder blades. True, he did so a little harder than necessary but the way she had said beau, as if he had as much appeal as a seven-day rash, kind of rubbed him the wrong way. He *could* be her beau if he wanted.

She stopped sputtering and shifted away from his patting, giving him a look fit to fry his brain.

"Wouldn't want you to choke to death," he said.

"I was in more danger of having a rib broke than choking." She moved with the determination of a filly eager for freedom. "I'm leaving now."

She didn't need to go away in a huff. He hadn't patted her *that* hard. He glanced around and realized the yard was emptying out. Lucy was already headed for the gate. Did she think to leave him standing in the middle of a vacant pen? He charged after her. "I'll see you home."

"I know the way. Probably better than you."

"I might be nothing but a rough, tough cowboy, but I'm gentleman enough to see a lady home."

"Perhaps you ought to go find yourself a lady, then."

He laughed. "You'll do."

She stopped so sharp he ploughed into her, staggered to keep his balance and steady her, too.

She spun about.

He winced back at the fiery light in her eyes. Had he said something offensive?

"I'll do? I'll do?" Her voice rose with every word.

"You don't think so?" How could she object to that? He'd meant it as admiration.

She clamped her lips together and continued down the street. Wade lifted his hands in confusion. Give him cows or horses any day over womenfolk. Who could understand them?

She stopped in front of the Dry Creek dining room. "This is where we part ways."

"You're going back to work?"

"No. I'm going to bed."

"In the dining room?"

She rolled her eyes. "I have a room in the back." She squinted at him as if suspecting shenanigans from him. "Right next to the room where Harry and Hettie sleep."

He grinned. "I had no plan to search out your sleeping quarters."

Her cheeks reddened. "I didn't suggest you did."

He kind of liked seeing her flustered. He shepherded his thoughts back to the reason he had looked her up. "I only want one thing from you."

She opened the door and stepped inside. "Good night." The door closed.

He raised his voice. "Don't you want to know why it's so important?"

Her muffled voice came through the wood. "There aren't enough words in the world to make me change my mind."

He stared at the closed door for some time before he whistled for the patient Two Bit and rode to his camp. A man with an ounce of sense would admit defeat and ride away, but he had made himself a promise to pay back Scout's kindness by bringing his daughter to visit. He wasn't about to give up. Lucy needed some persuading was all. And he was a patient man. He just hoped he wouldn't have to be too patient. He'd like to get back in time to see Scout before his friend departed this life.

He wondered how Scout was doing. Wade had arranged for an old cowboy friend to stay with Scout when he'd left to find Lucy. But Wade didn't figure Scout had many days left in him. He needed to hurry along Lucy's change of mind. He again prayed—a still unfamiliar activity. *God, help me accomplish the task I've chosen.*

Lucy shut her bedroom door and began to prepare for bed.

She didn't want to know anything more about her father. She'd spent too many pointless years waiting and hoping for him to do more than flit in and out of her life. She'd seen far too clearly how her mother had pined after a man who had made promises he never kept. After her mother died, still hoping for her father to make good on his promises, Lucy had sworn never to need or want anything more from her father. Nothing Wade could say or do would change that.

She sat cross-legged on her bed and opened her Bible. It had been her mother's. In the front were the family history pages. Lucy stared at them. Her name and birth date entered by her mother. Her mother's death in Lucy's handwriting. The births and dates of death of her mother's parents and her mother's brother who had died when he was only three months old. She turned to the conspicuously empty page for registering marriages. No marriage between her parents had ever been entered because her father failed to marry her mother and make an honest woman out of her, despite his many promises to do so.

Lucy sighed. It was old news. She no longer cared. Turning the pages carefully, she paused at the bookmark and read a chapter before gently replacing the Bible in its place of honor on her bedside table. She said her prayers as she'd done from her earliest remembrance. She knew—because her mother told her often—there had been a time when their lives didn't include churchgoing, Bible reading and prayer. A time when her mother had been a rebel and a runaway. But she thankfully did not recall that period. Her father was part of her mother's BC time—Before Christ—and Lucy did not want any share of it.

She lay staring at the narrow window high in the wall opposite her bed. Often she wished she could see outside without standing on her tiptoes, but Harry and Hettie were more than generous to provide her a room. She had only to think about Roy to realize her life without family might be a whole lot worse.

Thinking of Roy brought her thoughts round to Wade. No doubt after her rude dismissal he'd ridden out for wherever it was he headed. Made no difference to her. He was like a hundred other cowboys she saw.

Only—she regretfully admitted—no other cowboy had insisted on accompanying her to a recitation, nor admitted bold-faced how he missed his ma and her favorite poem.

She would doubtless never see him again and that, she told herself, was a good thing.

* * *

The next day was Sunday and Lucy headed out to church. Hettie and Harry had never asked her to work on Sunday. They had another gal come in to handle the Sunday crowd.

As she sat enjoying the organ music before the service began, someone slipped into the pew beside her. Wade!

She couldn't tell him to move along—not in church. Not that she didn't want to. But she feared she would incur the wrath of God if she acted on her unkind thoughts, so she gave him a smile that went no further than the corners of her mouth. Indeed, her lips said, "Good morning." But her eyes said something entirely different.

"Nice to see you at church," he whispered.

"You thought me a heathen, did you?"

He quirked an eyebrow. "Now why would you think such a thing?"

Why, indeed? But her conscience smote her. She'd been rude and dismissive. And him being a stranger in town. Hadn't the Lord commanded them to be careful to entertain strangers? A grin filled her mouth as she thought of the rest of the verse—entertaining angels unawares. She had her doubts about Wade being any sort of an angel.

"Care to share the cause of your amusement?" he whispered as the pews filled up around them.

She couldn't restrain herself and told him about

the verse. She then added, "It doesn't say what those who aren't angels turn out to be."

He managed to look sad even though his eyes shone with amusement. "I would not expect anyone to consider me an angel. But I guess that means you're obligated to entertain me this afternoon."

Obligated?

Her mind said no—she wanted nothing to do with a cowboy who knew her father and expected she would be glad to pay him a visit.

Her heart said otherwise. Obligation, cowboy, father—none of it mattered. The idea of an afternoon in this man's company sounded fine.

Her mouth said, "I guess I'm obligated."

He grinned. "I guess I am, too. No cowboy in his right mind would turn down such a generous invitation."

Knowing he realized as much as she that it had not been one bit generous, they both laughed. Seems he didn't mind the obligation any more than she, which was somehow all wrong. This man had made his intention perfectly clear—he only cared about spending time with her in order to persuade her to visit her father.

Just as she'd made it clear as a spring morning she wouldn't be persuaded. So, what harm was there in spending a sunny afternoon with him? It wasn't as if she was about to let this man, or any man, share anything but fragments of time. She had no need nor desire to give a man the right to twist her life into disarray as her father had done to her mother.

And herself.

She managed to postpone how she would deal with the afternoon until the service was over and she turned to see Wade grinning at her, his eyes dancing with amusement. She got the feeling he knew she'd boxed herself into a tight corner and he was enjoying her discomfort far too much for her liking.

She lifted her head. This was nothing she couldn't handle. "Let's get some lunch from the dining room." Hettie would willingly give them a portable lunch. Lucy thought she'd take him to the park where the young people tended to congregate on Sunday afternoons. Safety in numbers.

When they arrived at the dining room and she told Hettie what she wanted, the woman practically crowed. "Off to courting corner, are you?"

Lucy gave her a look of devout distaste, grateful Wade had waited outside, out of hearing distance. "I'm not interested in courting, only in having lots of people around so I don't have to personally amuse him."

Hettie chortled. "I suppose that's why all the other young people go there, too?"

"I wouldn't know."

"Now, don't get all prickly with me, Lucy gal. I recall a time or two you've been there with some anxious young man."

"I don't need a man."

"So you say. You'll change your mind soon enough when the right one comes along." She handed Lucy a basket full of food. "Now, off you go. Have fun. Who knows? This might be the right one."

Lucy thanked Hettie and waited until she was almost out the door to add, "Not in a million years." She'd never trust her happiness and future to any man.

Thanks to Hettie's comments, she felt conspicuous as she led Wade to the park where she was certain everyone she met had the same sly look in their eyes, and similar thoughts in their heads.

At least Wade had no idea how people viewed a harmless little jaunt to the park.

She saw a spot under a sprawling group of trees where several others she knew gathered. Mr. and Mrs. Nolan sat by themselves on a nearby bench. With three daughters of courting age, they usually spent the afternoon at the park, providing proper supervision.

"Over there." Lucy pointed toward the group.

"They your friends?" Wade looked toward a more secluded spot where an umbrella of branches provided an alarming amount of privacy. "It's quieter over there."

"They'll be glad to let us join them." She didn't give him a chance to say yea or nay. She had no intention of being shepherded to a place where they would be alone, knowing he would likely consider it an opportunity to tell her how she ought to visit her father. She led him to her choice of location and introduced him to the group—most of whom had been at church earlier. After a round of greetings, she found a roomy spot and allowed Wade to spread the blanket Hettie had put in the basket.

The afternoon heat made everyone mellow. Lucy was glad no one prodded her with questions about Wade. She didn't want to talk about him. She didn't want to explain who he was, what he was doing here.

Hettie had packed fried chicken and fresh buns for Lucy, which they'd both enjoyed. Lucy took out a plate of cookies and offered it to Wade.

He took one. "I see there are certain advantages to working in a dining room." He slanted an amused look toward the next couple who'd had only syrup sandwiches.

"I don't think they noticed." It was the youngest Nolan girl and a farm boy.

"If they did, they didn't seem to care." Wade leaned close. "I think they're more interested in their sparking."

His breath warmed her cheeks, filling her with a curious sense of longing.

She pushed away the idea. Only thing she longed for was her self-sufficiency. Life was meant to be

lived, enjoyed, embraced, not spent clasping hopeless
dreams based on empty promises from a man.

She would not be like her mother.

Wade still leaned close, his gaze warm as sun
flashing on a quiet lake, his expression curiously
watchful, as if wanting something from her.

She shifted away, turned to gather the remnants
of their lunch into the basket. She knew what he
wanted—for her to visit her father. But she wouldn't
do it. She'd already given her father too many chances,
wasted too many hopes and dreams on him.

Lawrence, a young man who seemed to escort a
different gal to the park every week, picked up his
guitar and began to pluck out a tune. He had a liking
for popular ballads, which made him a hit with both
sexes. He began to sing "Oh! Susanna." Soon, more
young people crowded around, joining their voices
to his as he went from one popular tune to another.

Lucy loved the songs and joined right in. She
didn't have to look directly at Wade to see he wasn't
singing. At first she thought he didn't know the newer
songs, but even when they sang some old hymns he
didn't join. She tried to remember if he'd sung at
church, but she'd been too busy mentally kicking
herself for agreeing to spend the afternoon with him
to pay attention.

She focused on the next song, and tried not to think
of Wade sitting there quietly. He shifted, stretched
out his legs, and leaned back on his right elbow. Was

he bored? Restless? Through some perverse idea that God wanted her to entertain this stranger, she'd volunteered her afternoon. If Wade chose to be not entertained by the music, that wasn't her problem. She'd done all that could be expected of her.

He sat up straight and pulled his knees to his chin. She didn't miss how he shuffled about so he could stare at her.

"An angel wouldn't stare," she whispered.

"You've known a few, have you?"

"No. But I know they wouldn't."

"Well, see, I'm not so sure. I think they watch us all the time."

She rolled her eyes to signify how silly she considered this conversation.

"Let's go for a walk." He bounced to his feet and held out a hand before she could refuse. She automatically let him pull her to her feet but withdrew from his grasp before they had gone two steps.

They headed past Mr. and Mrs. Nolan. Mrs. Nolan was writing a letter. Mr. Nolan was lying in the shade, his hat pulled over his eyes.

Lucy waited until they were far enough away from the music to be able to converse easily before she spoke. "I noticed you didn't sing."

"If you heard me you'd know for sure I was no angel." His tone carried a hint of self-mockery. "Cowboys normally sing to the cattle at night to calm them. I tried it once. The cows all signed a petition requesting I stop."

She laughed at the idea of cows signing a piece of paper. "Did they read it for you, too?"

"Read it myself but the head cow stepped on my foot to emphasize the point." He paused to rub at the toe of his boot as if his foot still hurt.

She laughed harder at his silliness. "It can't be that bad."

"Oh, yes it can."

Now she wanted nothing more than to hear and judge for herself. "Show me."

He held up his hands as if warning her. "I don't want the afternoon to end on a sour note. Or a flat one."

"You think I'd run home if I heard you sing?"

"I know you would, with your ears covered, begging me to stop."

He kept a deadpan expression so she couldn't know for sure how serious he was but she couldn't believe he meant all he said.

She held a hand up as if swearing honesty before a court of law. "I vow I would not run away if you sang."

Their gazes locked and for one still moment, nothing existed apart from the two of them and the promise of something exciting between them.

"Would you run for some other reason?" His words were low and soft, teasing.

She tried to find an answer to his question. "I can't say." At that moment, she could think of nothing that would send her running. Not when her heart had developed a sudden ache to know more about him.

He took her hand.

She let him.

They reached the edge of the park but didn't turn around. Instead, they crossed the street, walked the half block to the edge of town and continued along the dusty road bordered by yellowed grass swaying in the breeze.

"This country is as flat as pie dough rolled out," he said.

"Great for farming, they say. Best number one hard wheat grown right here. Much of it on bonanza farms. Can you imagine one farm with thousands of acres under crop? I'd like to see that some day." Why was she running over at the mouth about farming? Only thing she knew about it was what she overheard at the dining room where some of the big landowners met with bankers and investors to discuss things.

Wade made a dismissive noise. "Farming is okay. But for real pretty scenery you should see ranching country. When I see the hills and trees and vast stretches of grass, I just want to put down roots like a big old cottonwood tree and never leave."

Lucy turned to stare at him. "I never knew a cowboy who wanted to settle down."

Wade gave an embarrassed grin and shrugged.

"Never thought about it like that but now you mention it, the idea sounds kind of nice. But the ranch I mean belongs to your father."

She pulled her hand from his grasp.

"Lucy, he's sick. Near death. All you have to do is visit him. How hard can that be?"

She backed away with every word he uttered. Her eyes felt overheated, the air too heavy to breathe. "I will never visit him."

"Why not?"

"Because when my mother died I decided I would no longer allow him any part of my life. He hurt her time and again with empty promises. I won't let him do the same thing to me."

"Just a little visit."

"Never."

Wade's jaw muscles flexed. "He's very sick."

"I'm sorry." She headed back to town like she was trying to outrun a thunderstorm.

He easily caught up to her. "I'll not leave until you change your mind."

"It will never happen." She mentally kicked herself all the way back to the dining room and slipped into her room. How many times had she vowed not to let her heart yearn for any man—not her father, and certainly not a run-of-the-mill cowboy? She wouldn't let herself care if the King of Spain showed up to court her. No. Her heart belonged to no one. Ever.

She'd witnessed the incredible pain and suffering in her mother's life and would have no part of it.

Yet she'd let her conscience, her duty, the warm sun and a pair of bright blue eyes momentarily make her forget.

Well, not again. Besides, Wade was only spending time with her in hopes of talking her into visiting her father. Wade said he was sick, dying even. But he'd been dead to her for years so what did it matter? Any little pang of remorse she felt was only for what she had once wanted.

And never had.

Chapter Three

Wade alternately stared at the ashes of his campfire and the dusty toes of his boots. Three days. Three long days he'd hung about trying to convince Lucy to do her duty as a daughter and a decent human being and visit her father before he died.

Wade had haunted the dining room waiting for opportunities to talk to Lucy until Harry had stomped out with a spoon the size of a bucket hanging from his ham-hock fists and ordered him to leave Lucy alone.

Wade had no desire to come to blows with the larger man or any of his primitive kitchen utensils, so he'd waited for an opportunity to speak to Lucy away from the eagle eyes of Harry.

He'd found such opportunity when he watched her and Roy settle on a rough plank bench in the shade of the livery stable. He followed at a distance, undetected, and slipped around the barn until he could listen and watch unobserved. It took him a moment to realize Lucy and Roy were bent over a book, their heads almost touching as Lucy taught the boy to read.

Huh. Wade sank back on his heels. Why would she spend that much time with Roy yet refuse to visit Scout—her own flesh and blood?

He moseyed around the corner and confronted the pair.

Roy glowered at him. "She don't want to see you. Thought she made that plain."

Wade wanted to laugh at the boy's belligerence. He posed no threat, carried no oversize kitchen spoon but he was every bit as protective of Lucy as Harry was. Having no desire to mock the boy's spirit, Wade kept his face expressionless. "I think she owes me a chance to explain."

Roy jumped to his feet, fists curled at his side and donned a scowl fit to curdle Wade's supper.

Lucy rose to Roy's side and dropped an arm across the boy's shoulders. "Let it be, Roy. I can defend myself." The way she stuck out her chin and gave Wade a look fit to set his hair on fire made him squirm.

"No need to get all prickly around me. I mean no harm."

"Just going to make a nuisance of yourself because you won't take no for an answer."

He thought some on that. Finally, he let out a long-suffering sigh. "I guess there's no point in hanging around any longer. 'Sides, I'd like to see Scout before he passes. You'll find me camped in that piddly patch of trees on the other side of town if you change your mind or decide you want to hear why I think the man deserves a visit from you." He purposely waited, hoping she'd be curious to know why he owed the man this, but she just stared.

"Fine." He spun around and marched away without a backward look, without saying all the hot words that pushed at the top of his head. The woman was a lost cause. Too bad for Scout, but perhaps it was best the man yearn after a girl he remembered as sweet and loving rather than face the truth about her coldheartedness.

He'd ride out first light. Or maybe he'd endure a train ride as he'd planned to do when he figured to have Lucy with him. He wanted to make it back in time to bid Scout farewell.

Though he hated to face the man and admit he'd failed to get Lucy to accompany him.

Even though he'd prayed. Guess a man couldn't expect God to jump to do his bidding. Being rescued by prayer once was more than most ever experienced and he would never forget the occasion, nor how it had made his faith in God grow like desert flowers after rain.

It was an experience that meant a lot to him. He

might have shared the details with Lucy in the hopes it would convince her to visit Scout.

God, I know I ain't got the right to ask for more than what You've already given, but if You could do something to prod Lucy to consider allowing Scout to see her once more before he dies...

He returned to his campsite and settled back against one of the puny trees. He'd wait until morning to leave. Give Lucy a chance to reconsider. Give God a chance to do something to persuade her.

Dusk turned the street gray and darkened the shadows along the buildings to indigo. Grasshoppers and crickets sought to outdo each other in their creaky nightly chorus. Birds settled in for the night, calling to each other one last time.

Lucy and Roy leaned against the livery stable wall. The worn wood hoarded the heat of the day and baked their backs, but they were too content to move. She'd been reluctant to return to her solitary room after the way Wade had stalked off, anger evident in every step. Her heart clenched. Seems Wade had found friendship, perhaps belonging, maybe even a home with her father—something she had wanted most of her life. But her wanting had brought her nothing but disappointment and pain. She would not let Wade's insistence and pleading trick her into walking headlong into a repeat of those emotions.

She should return to her room. If Harry and Hettie

knew she was out alone after dark they would both scold her. But she wasn't exactly alone. Roy had no place to go but the corner of the loft where he slept, so he willingly kept her company.

They had no need to talk but sat in companionable silence listening to the night and bits of conversation floating on the still air.

A harsher, louder sound caused them both to jolt upright.

"It's just the door into the barn," Lucy said.

Angry voices rose and fell. She made out a few words. "Cheat." "Pay back."

Curious as to what it was about, Lucy looked around, saw a tiny circle of yellow light and pressed her eye to the hole in the wall. Roy found another spot. From her spy hole Lucy got a clear view of Smitty. She resisted the urge to spit. Smitty was a scoundrel and the town could well do without him. He bullied and threatened his way around, acting like he owned the town and its inhabitants. He spent time in jail on a semiregular basis for minor offenses. Too bad someone couldn't prove one of the many bigger things they suspected him of.

Another man faced Smitty, someone Lucy had seen only a time or two. She'd noticed the man had eyes that seemed to see everything, yet reveal nothing. But he sure looked scared right now. He held his hands out toward Smitty.

"I got no gun."

That's when Lucy saw that Smitty held a pistol aimed straight at the other man's heart.

Her breath stalled halfway to her lungs and she clawed for Roy's hand but found nothing but raw, slivered boards. She should leave. Run as far and fast as she could but she seemed tacked to the wall watching the two men, their forms wavering uncertainly in the flickering lamplight.

Smitty's teeth gleamed in a sneer. "Dead men tell no tales." Light flared from the end of his pistol and the noise of a gunshot rattled against the walls.

The second man clutched at his chest. He stared at his blood-covered hands, then gave Smitty a look of surprise before he pitched to the ground.

"Is he dead?" Roy whispered.

Smitty, who had leaned over to put a second gun in the fallen man's hand, glanced toward them.

"Shh." Lucy didn't dare move for fear of giving away their presence.

Smitty stepped back, turned to a third man that Lucy hadn't seen until this point. She recognized him, too. Smitty's half-brained sidekick, Louie. The man wore a perpetual smile that revealed a whole lot more meanness than humor.

Smitty spoke to the man and nodded toward Lucy and Roy's position. Louie jerked his head in compliance and strode for the door.

Lucy's blood burned through her body. "They know we're here." She turned, grabbed Roy's hand in a death grip, held her skirts with her other hand and ran like her life depended on it, which she was quite sure it did. They didn't stop until they crossed behind the blacksmith shop where they pressed to the wall. Lucy held her breath hoping they hadn't been spotted. She hoped they were invisible. She prayed the men might think they'd been mistaken in thinking someone had seen them.

"Who's there?" Louie called.

Lucy clutched at Roy's hand knowing he was as scared as she.

"Maybe I seen a kid and maybe someone else. Thought it was a woman."

Lucy's heart rattled against her ribs. *Please, God, let them think they made a mistake.*

"It's that kid who sleeps here," Smitty grumbled. "And I know who the girl is. Only one person spends any time with the kid. Never mind them now. We know where to find them. We'll get you later," he called.

Lucy knew he meant the words for them just as surely as she knew he wouldn't hesitate to do to them the same thing he'd done to that man in the barn.

Other voices called. She recognized the sheriff's voice asking what happened.

She leaned over her knees and tried to catch her breath.

"What we gonna do?"

"Let me think." They had a few minutes while

the sheriff investigated, but she knew Smitty had set it up to look like self-defense when it was clear and simple murder. Only Roy and Lucy knew the truth. And Louie, who would never tell. He'd probably been cheering in the background when Smitty shot the unarmed man.

Her heart rate spiked again. Smitty wouldn't hesitate to get rid of anyone who could testify against him.

How long would it take for everyone to accept Smitty's version of what transpired? How long did it give her to come up with a plan of escape?

"Come on." She practically dragged Roy toward the dining room. They couldn't stay there. It would be the first place Smitty would look. All he had to do was wait for her to…

Her heart climbed up her throat and clawed at the back of her mouth.

"Hurry. We have to find someplace to hide." She burst into her room and grabbed up her Bible, which held her meager life savings in an envelope. She grabbed a battered valise Hettie had given her and randomly threw some articles of clothing on top of her Bible having no idea where she would go. She only knew that it wasn't safe here.

She headed for the door, paused. She didn't want Hettie and Harry to worry so she scribbled a note and left it on her pillow. "Went to visit my father. Will contact you later."

It was an excuse they would believe.

"What are we gonna do?" Roy's voice thinned with fear.

She grabbed his hand. "Follow me." She had no plan except escape.

They slipped out of her room and clung to the black shadows as they made their way to the edge of town opposite the livery barn. A commotion indicated the sheriff was still investigating along with every curious citizen who had come running at the sound of a gunshot.

Smitty wouldn't be able to look for them until that was settled.

Roy yanked away. "If we're leaving, I'm taking Queenie." Mr. Peterson had given Roy an old nag of a horse. Roy diligently tethered her where she could nibble grass and faithfully carried water to her.

"Roy, we don't have time."

"We could ride her."

There was something to that. "Where is she?"

He named a place and they head in that direction. "We'll stop and get her."

They just might get away in time.

Two Bit whinnied.

"What is it, boy?" Wade tipped his head and listened. He heard it a minute later—the sound of an approaching rider.

He scooped up his rifle and lounged with deceptive

casualness. In his experience only trouble came riding into camp before dawn.

"Wade, are you there?"

His heart skidded sideways and crashed into his ribs. "Lucy, is that you?" What was she doing out before the sky had begun to lighten?

She rode up to him.

He grabbed the bridle of her horse, all the time alert for signs of danger. When he saw none, he relaxed. "You've decided to come with me?" he teased. She'd made it abundantly clear wild horses and six mad bulls wouldn't drag her to the ranch.

"On one condition."

He wished he could see her better. Assure himself she was teasing because, plain and simple, he didn't believe she meant it.

"Yeah." His voice dripped with sarcasm.

"Wade, I mean it. I'll go with you to see my father if you agree—" She glanced over her shoulder. Roy peeked around her arm. "You agree to take Roy."

Wade wasn't much for fancy talk. Sometimes he had to search for words. It came from spending most of his waking hours with nothing but cows, horses and equally untalkative cowboys. But for the life of him he couldn't find even one word in his surprised brain. Not one word to say to this gal who had changed her mind faster than Dakota weather.

"Wade, we'll go with you. But we have to hurry."

Her urgent tone caused his brain to burst into a gallop.

"What's the rush?" He could feel the nervous tension vibrating from the pair. No way was he taking a step anywhere until he knew what was going on.

"I'll tell you everything on the way."

No mistaking the way her voice quivered. He guessed it was fear or nervousness. "What's the hurry?"

"Smitty is after us."

He knew about Smitty. Anyone who had been in town more than a few hours knew of the man. Either by word of mouth or by encounter. Wade had seen him in the store a couple of days ago. Had been forced to witness the man blatantly threaten a farmer over some disputed fence line. From what Wade gathered, the farmer was within his rights but it was plain as dirt on a white shirt that Smitty didn't care about what was right. And certainly didn't intend to let it interfere with his plans.

After the pair left, he asked the store owner why the sheriff didn't do something. The man said, "He'd like to, but so far no one will testify against Smitty."

"He's gonna kill us." Roy's voice shook. All the kid's bravado had vanished.

Roy's fear sent Wade's nerves into full alert. "Why?"

"Smitty killed a man in cold blood. We saw him.

Smitty doesn't want any witnesses." Lucy's voice trembled so bad he wanted to scoop her from the horse and hold her tight, assure her he'd keep her safe.

"You going to help or just stare at the horse's nostrils?"

Wade laughed. "Lucy gal, you sure do have a sweet way of asking."

"Phweet. If I'd known you expected sweet talk I'd give it, but right now I think urgency is a little more important."

"Why don't we just to tell the sheriff the truth?"

"You don't know Smitty." Her voice was tight, signaling her fear. "He'll convince everyone the shooting was self-defense. He'll already have half a dozen men as nasty as him watching for us. We wouldn't make it two steps in town before he or one of them would grab us. We wouldn't get anywhere near the sheriff." Her words grew more urgent. "The best thing we can do is go somewhere and hide."

"I expect you're right. Good thing I was ready to go." He settled the saddle on Two Bit, stuck his rifle in the boot and swung up. He paused to have a good look at the other horse in the gray light. "Where did you find that old nag?"

"She's a good old horse." Roy sounded a whole lot more like himself as he defended the bag of bones.

"Emphasis on old," Wade muttered. "Come on, let's make tracks." The "good old horse" would have found Roy a load let alone the pair of them. She probably found her skin almost more'n she could handle. He edged up beside Lucy. "Roy, get on behind me. We'll have to take turns carrying you."

Just a few hours ago Wade had asked God to melt Lucy's stubbornness. Little did he expect things to turn around so suddenly or in such an alarming fashion. He scanned the horizon, saw no sign of pursuit and prayed for God's protection. He briefly considered his options. Seems he had only two—head for the train, or ride west. Riding left them exposed and vulnerable. He could likely outride and outmaneuver any pursuers, but doubted Lucy or Roy were up to the challenge. Certainly not on the old nag they had brought along.

On the other hand, he'd picked a campsite on the far side of town away from the rail station. Didn't make any sense to ride through town.

He made up his mind. They'd head for the railway but not through town.

"Let's ride." He urged Two Bit into an easy lope. They rode from the shelter of the trees and headed west. A few minutes later, he glanced over his shoulder to check Lucy's progress.

She kicked at the old horse's side and slapped at the animal with the end of the reins. The horse managed what might pass for a jog.

"I can walk faster than that." Someone had not gotten a good bargain on horseflesh.

He waited for the struggling pair to catch up. Lucy looked about ready to chew a handful of nails for breakfast. "Where did you get that old hay burner?"

The look she shot him made him winch. "Mr. Peterson gave her to Roy."

He sputtered with surprise then the humor of it hit him and he roared with laughter. Two Bit perked up his ears and danced sideways. Roy clung to his waist. Wade wiped his eyes and continued laughing despite Lucy's pinched look.

"Did you think we stole her?" she demanded.

Wade managed to choke back his enjoyment of the idea of someone persuading Roy he was doing him a favor though he couldn't stop it from circling his words as he spoke. "Mr. Peterson saved himself the price of a bullet and left Roy with the responsibility of feeding the old thing. Got to admire a man with such business savvy." Even free was too much for this sorry piece of horseflesh. He whooped with laughter.

Lucy fixed him with a hard, unyielding frown.

Wade forced himself to put on a sober face, though inside he continued to chortle. "If we hurry we might make the rail station by nightfall." He reined toward his destination, knowing now he could hope for nothing more than a plodding walk.

The pair of them seemed to think a walking glue factory was a wondrous gift. It amazed him.

Delighted him. Filled him with admiration for the kind of spunk his Lucy showed.

His? Was his brain addled from surprise and too much laughter? She wasn't his. Never would be. She had only agreed to accompany him because she needed to get away from Smitty. Would she stay on the ranch any longer than it took to say "Hello, Father. Goodbye, Father.?" Then reality hit him square between his eyes. Lucy couldn't ride away after a hurried goodbye. Not until Smitty had been locked behind bars. The idea of that man posing a threat to Lucy or Roy made his fists coil.

They inched across the flat prairie. Although he took a circuitous route that kept him away from town, he felt as exposed as the sun. His skin itched at how easy it would be for someone to spot them and ride after them. Running from pursuers was impossible. But getting back to Dry Creek and catching the train was equally impossible. By the time they got there, Smitty would have every way in and out of town guarded by one of his cohorts.

He pulled up. "This ain't going to work."

Lucy's shoulders drew back. "Where there's a will, there's a way."

He chuckled at her determination. "You planning to push that nag all the way across Dakota?"

Her eyes sparkled. "Now, how gentlemanly would that be? If someone is to push…" She left the rest unsaid. But he understood her message. If anyone had to do the pushing, she expected it to be him.

He eyed the tired old horse. "I could try riding her. Maybe I could convince her to go a little faster. Otherwise, we'll be spending the winter out in the open plain."

Lucy scowled. "You'd whip her, I suppose?"

Roy dropped to the ground and rushed to the old nag's side. "You can't hit her. She can't help if she's old."

"Don't suppose either of you thought to bring wheels?"

Two pairs of eyes regarded him suspiciously.

"The way I see it..." He pushed his hat back on his head and leaned over the saddle horn as if contemplating one of the universe's darkest mysteries. "Either we plan to inch across the prairie—easy for anybody to see us, easier for them to chase us down—or we put wheels under that thing and I'll drag her."

"'Course we didn't bring any wheels."

He sighed. "I feared that might be your answer. Like I said, this isn't going to work."

They all stared at the horse.

"She happen to have a name?" Somehow, it might be easier to deal with her if she was more than a nameless pile of skin draped over protruding bones.

Roy wrapped his arm around the sorry animal's

head. " 'Course she has a name. It's Queenie. 'Cause she's like a queen." His tone dared Wade to question the name.

In order to restrain his laughter, Wade drew his lips in tight hoping he looked thoughtful. He slanted a look at Lucy and when he saw her eyes brimming with merriment, he had to bite the inside of his lip.

But their lack of speed was no laughing matter. They had to find some other way of getting across this open land. He studied the landscape trying to come up with a solution. Wheels were not the answer. Unless...he stared southwest. "We'll go that way."

"We aren't going back, are we?"

"Lucy, we're going to find some wheels."

"Who's going to push?"

"The iron horse."

"A train?"

"Yup." He'd planned on catching the new SOO line that was direct to Minot and from there they would ride. But if he dropped down to the Northern Pacific line and the less direct route, it might serve their purpose even better, make it a little harder for any pursuers to know for sure where they were headed. And the line was considerably closer if his reckoning was right.

Lucy brightened faster than the sun that now sat several degrees above the horizon, promising another searing day.

Wade eyed the flat land. Being out on the

unprotected prairie didn't seem like the best plan a man could devise. "Come on, Roy. Climb on." He reached out a hand.

"Will we get breakfast when we get there? I'm awfully hungry."

"Roy, you're always hungry." Lucy's tone warned him not to complain.

Wade lifted the boy to the back of his horse. "I'm feeling kind of hollow myself. I'm sure we'll be able to rustle up something." If he was correct they should connect about the same place as the little town of Anders. They'd find food there. Plus water and relief from the unrelenting heat.

Three hours later, the heat shimmered unmercifully and between them they had downed his entire supply of water.

Wade began to wonder if they'd missed the line entirely and were doomed to wither into nothingness in the baked grass.

Chapter Four

❧

The hat Lucy wore did little to provide adequate shade. The sun was unrelenting, threatening to bake the three of them. She'd watched Roy swallow the last of the water what seemed an hour ago but was likely only a few minutes. Roy had long since stopped complaining about hunger. He no longer mentioned the heat. In fact, he looked about ready to perish. And she felt the same. Did Wade have any idea where they were or was he, as she suspected, only guessing? She kicked Queenie mercilessly until she rode at Wade's side. "How much farther?"

"Can't be far."

"Seems I heard that a time or two already."

"It's closer than last time you asked."

She sighed mightily, too hot to hide her worry. "So is Christmas. I'm wondering which will get here first."

"I 'spect we would have been there by now except we have to move at a snail's pace thanks to Queenie there." Sarcasm edged his words. "A mistake if I ever saw one."

"Would you suggest we should have hung around making detailed plans until Smitty found us?"

"'Course not. But next time steal a fast horse."

Roy tipped sideways and Wade caught him. "Hang on, Roy, we're almost there."

"We're already *there.*" Lucy's lips pursed as she spoke. "Which is where? Lost in the middle of nowhere. Going round in circles waiting for the buzzards to find us."

"We ain't lost. We ain't going in circles."

"I suppose you mean that to be comforting? It's not."

"Look yonder." He pointed.

She squinted into the distance. "Nothing but more heat waves and endless grass."

"Right down on the horizon. See. A water tower. It's our destination."

She finally located it. Her whole insides kicked with new hope. She checked over her shoulder and allowed herself to relax when she saw no dust trailing in their direction. "Roy, hear that? We're almost there. Thank God."

Roy stirred himself. "I'm thirsty."

Wade patted Roy's leg. "There'll be water there. And food."

Now that her inner knot of concern had relaxed, Lucy's conscience smote her. Wade had led them to safety. And she'd been snippy about how long it took when really she had only one party to blame— Queenie, the slowest moving horse this side of eternity. "Wade, I'm sorry for being impatient."

He slowed so they rode side by side and gave her a look of wide-eyed surprise. "Why Lucy, I hardly noticed."

Her heart kicked up its pace at his teasing.

"Besides, I intend to get you safely to the ranch."

His words effectively reminded her he had only one reason to care about her safety—his own feelings for a man she didn't want to see. His concern wasn't personal at all, much as her fickle brain hoped for just a fraction of a second it was. Which was stupid. She'd long ago learned not to pin her hopes and heart on expecting anything from a man.

And now she had to face the reality of seeing the one person she'd vowed to never speak to again— her father. She looked at Roy, now alert and peering toward the approaching town. She hadn't been able to see an alternative in the predawn hours. After a moment's thought she could still find none.

Somehow she'd survive the visit and return to her familiar world and her own plans. She only hoped it would be with her emotions unscathed. But as she allowed herself a fleeting glance at Wade who continued to study the horizon with a mixture of relief and concern, Lucy knew walking away with her heart intact may well be impossible. Not only would her father shred it yet again, she feared Wade would, as well.

It took them another hour to reach the town. They went directly to the low building that served as the train station and learned the next train would arrive in half an hour. That gave them enough time to hustle up some food and drink.

Half an hour later, their thirst quenched and hunger demands met, she and Roy stepped into the puffing, smoke-belching train.

Lucy heaved a sigh of relief as she sank down on a stiff green leather seat. Roy guarded the sack of sandwiches wrapped in brown paper Wade had ordered for the trip. He didn't intend to let anything happen to their food supply. She glanced out the window and allowed a bit of tension to ease from her muscles. So far there'd been no sign of Smitty. He didn't appear to have followed them on horseback or he would have overtaken them.

Not that she was foolish enough to expect he'd forget she and Roy were witnesses to his murderous act.

Wade had been seeing to the horses and now joined them.

She spread her dusty skirts and hugged the middle of the bench. As if reading her reluctance and finding it amusing, Wade grinned, pushed aside her skirts and planted himself beside her. She shifted over and pressed against the window trying to convince herself she had no reason to be annoyed at him. After all, he had readily agreed to protect them. Of course, she knew it was only because he had gotten what he came for.

No, the reason she was annoyed was because she'd agreed to go with him after days of vowing nothing would drag her out to the beautiful ranch. But she had only his word that it wasn't a spit-dry piece of land with nothing to break the monotony of the endless prairie.

She had only hours before she came face-to-face with her father.

As if sensing her regret at being in the very position she'd vowed to avoid, Wade leaned close. "Relax, Lucy. Enjoy the journey."

Annoyed because he'd read her thoughts, she jerked back and faced him. "It's a little difficult knowing what's at the end."

He considered her for a moment then a slow smile filled his eyes with sunshine. "Lucy, you might be surprised at what you find."

She wanted to argue but he stared out the window, a dreamy look on his face and spoke before she could gather her thoughts.

"It's a real pretty place and there's lots of room to roam. No need to spend time in anyone's company unless you chose to. There's one place— You ride up this slope that seems like nothing more than a ripple in the prairie. But when you reach the top you realize you've climbed a small mountain. You can see for miles and miles. They say the Indians used it as a place to spot game and enemies." He sucked in air like a man deprived of it for most of a day. "You can't help but be impressed. When we get there I'll show you."

She wondered what it would be like to have such a view. And something inside her reached for the experience.

Then he met her watchful, wondering gaze and gave a self-deprecating chuckle. "I do go on, don't I?"

She nodded. "You sound like a man in love."

He lowered his gaze. "Guess you could say I am." Slowly he faced her again. "I thank you for agreeing to come."

"It's only to get away from Smitty. I still don't want to see my father."

He nodded, his expression regretful and then glanced across to the facing seat. "Roy boy has fallen asleep."

They smiled at the boy who was curled up, his dark lashes resting on his cheeks, his fists still tightly clutching the bag of sandwiches.

All morning, under the hot sun, Wade had kept his thoughts centered on getting them to safety. He hadn't allowed himself to think past the immediate need to reach the rail line.

Now he couldn't keep his fears and anger at bay as he pictured Smitty trying to chase down Lucy and Roy. Hoping to disguise his concern, he stretched his legs under the seat where Roy slept and crossed his arms as if nothing mattered more than enjoying the trip.

"When did you see this—?" He left the question unfinished having no desire to scratch any itchy ears of the nearby passengers. "Where did you spend the night?"

"It was already dark when…it happened."

What was she doing out after dark? A woman with a speck of sense would be home safe and sound at that time. But he refrained from saying so, knowing Lucy would get all prickly and defensive and likely not tell him the things he wanted to know.

"I knew Smitty would look for us at the dining room. So we couldn't stay there." Despite the heat, she shivered.

It was all he could do to keep his arms crossed instead of reaching for her and pulling her against his chest. She didn't deserve to be involved in Smitty's messy schemes. Nor did Roy.

"Roy wouldn't leave Queenie behind." She chuckled. "I know she's no prize—"

"You could say that again with all honesty."

"But it's about the only thing Roy has ever owned. It makes him feel special to have a horse."

Wade understood that. Roy didn't have much reason to feel valued. A man had to be something at least in his own mind. Guess owning a horse—no matter how sorry—did that for Roy.

"We went to where Queenie was tethered and led her farther from town then sat down to catch our breath and try to think. Only thing I could think of was joining up with you." She slid him a sideways glance and a tiny smile tugged at the corner of her lips.

The look said so many things; her regret at having no other choice, and maybe—if he let himself push the meaning of her smile—just a hint of gladness that she didn't.

He forced his gaze to the window across the aisle and watched the prairie slip by broken only by the occasional settler's shack. He wanted her to be glad but had no reason at all to believe she was. He'd been her only option. Nothing more.

"Wade, what's to stop Smitty from checking who got on the train? Wouldn't take more than a question or two to locate us."

He gladly reined his thoughts back to a situation where he had some hope of making a difference. "I've thought of that. If we head to Minot there will be lots of different routes we can take. Maybe we'll get on a train and let him think we headed one direction then get off and backtrack before we head for the ranch." Pretty hard to completely hide their activities, but with a bit of good fortune and some help from the Mighty Lord they might slip away.

"You'll be safe," Wade promised. "Both of you." This could get pricey. It was a good thing he'd brought a fat wallet.

She shifted so she could give him a hard look. "Don't make promises you can't keep. Smitty is an evil man who won't easily let us get away." She shivered and jerked back to stare out the window.

Wade curled fists into his armpits.

"Still, I won't stay any longer than I need to," she murmured.

He knew she referred to her visit to the ranch and Scout. "You won't be safe back in Dry Creek. Not while Smitty is walking about a free man. No, Lucy, you'll have to hole up at the ranch until it's safe to leave." He slouched lower in the seat happy to have settled the matter satisfactorily in his mind.

She stifled a groan. "Don't see why you're looking so happy about it. My life has been turned inside out."

For a moment he didn't answer as he sought for words that would say all the things he felt in his heart. "Sometimes change is good. Surprises can turn into prizes."

"Don't get all philosophical on me, Wade Miller."

He bristled and pulled himself upright. "Don't you go getting all prickly."

"Prickly? Me?" Even as she spoke, her defensive barriers came up.

"You got something against men in general or just your pa?" He knew the question would turn her into a porcupine but he was past caring. Past trying to avoid the topics he wanted most to talk about.

"Neither." Her voice growled with denial. Then she laughed. "Maybe both."

"Maybe it's time you got over it."

They dueled with their eyes. Hers flashed lightning. He guessed his reflected it back with added vigor. "You got no reason to resent me. Didn't I just save your skin? Didn't I just promise to protect you?"

She glowered.

"And no matter what Scout did to start this silent war of yours, he deserves a visit from you at the very least. After all, he is your father."

"He never married my mother," she mumbled.

"Huh?" Scout had forgotten to mention that little detail. What else had he left out? "Don't change the fact he's your pa."

"My father," she corrected as if there was a vast difference.

"When did you last see him?"

She shifted and stared out the window, her eyes narrowed as she squinted against the bright sun. He guessed it wasn't the sun that made her pull her lips into a tight line. "He didn't even bother coming to my mother's funeral."

"Likely he didn't know." Scout hadn't said so just as he'd never mentioned he hadn't married Lucy's mother and he guessed he must have known that for sure.

"I sent a wire. He knew. He just didn't care enough to stir himself and make a trip. He only came when and if it suited him."

Wade tried to think what would make the man decide to visit or not. What constituted something suitable? For the life of him he couldn't think what would keep a man away from his family. Why if he had a little girl like Lucy or—he licked his lips and tried to stall the thought but it came without pause—a wife like Lucy, he couldn't imagine what could keep him away.

He shifted his thoughts back to Scout and safer territory. What she said about Scout simply did not fit with what he knew of the man. "Maybe he's changed."

She gave another sound of disbelief. Between the way her eyes flashed and the expressive sounds she made, Lucy had no need of words. He read her message loud and clear.

"My mother died when I was fourteen. How old were you?" He wanted to talk of things that didn't bring out the prickles in her.

"I was sixteen."

"What did you do?"

"I was a mother's helper for a couple of years then I met a friend of Hettie's and she arranged for me to work for Harry and Hettie."

He didn't like to think of her all alone especially when she had family who wanted her. Didn't seem right. "I barely remember my pa. He was killed in an accident when I was eight." He widened his eyes to keep from closing them where he knew he would see the pictures of that day branded on the inside of his eyelids. "They brought him home strapped over the back of a horse." His voice cracked and he stopped. Forced his eyes to see the passing scenery out the window across the aisle.

A warm hand touched his elbow. "Wade, it sounds awful. I'm sorry."

She withdrew her hand but her touch lingered in his pores, in his thoughts, bringing with it a breath of comfort.

"So, you were alone at fourteen. What did you do?"

"I was used to being alone by then."

"But your mother—?"

He hadn't meant to say that. It sounded as if he didn't miss Ma. He had. He did. "Ma had to work after Pa died. She got a job as housekeeper but the people didn't want a dirty little boy hanging about."

Lucy bristled up as if poked by a stick. "I'm sure you weren't dirty."

Seeing her all defensive on his behalf spread sugar over the mean comments he'd endured from the Collins family. "Ma scrubbed me with a brush and washed my clothes within an inch of survival."

"There you go. You weren't a dirty little boy at all."

His grin spread like butter on hot bread. "Nope. But I learned to stay out of sight. Unless they needed me to run an errand. Then suddenly I was Wade, the useful boy." He raised his voice in a high mimic of Mrs. Collins who said that very thing when she needed him.

Lucy widened her eyes. "They sound like a delightful family." Then she giggled. "Sorry for my sarcasm. Hettie is always telling me it isn't an attractive attribute in a young woman."

Wade couldn't stop staring. Couldn't stop thinking how good it felt to share his past with Lucy. "I guess it's like dynamite. Good in small doses."

She laughed outright at that and something sweeter than sugar edged across his heart. "I'll have to keep that in mind." She turned to look out the window again.

Wade slowly eased his world back toward normal but before he reached that state she jerked back to face him. "So, what did you do? All alone. Really alone."

"Found work. I spent some time working in a store. Worked on a farm then got on driving cows. Sure saw some pretty country doing that."

"Yeah?" Her eyes widened. "Like what?"

He told her about Texas, about the Canadian foot-hills. "It's real pretty up in the British Territories. Snow caps on the mountains most of the year."

She drank in his words as if she saw the things he described.

He liked the way she shifted to watch him. He liked the way her eyes sparkled as he talked about the scenery he'd seen. He especially liked the way she held his gaze as if every word he spoke meant more than gold to her. "Late last fall I was on my way south. Hoped to cross the prairie and make it to Texas before winter. But I was barely into the Dakotas when the temperature dropped like a rock. I could feel snow in the air and looked around for shelter." He chuckled. "Couldn't find myself so much as a tree to cling to. So I kept riding. Hoping I'd run into some-thing. All I ran into was a snowstorm." He paused to enjoy the way her eyes widened. "I was lost for sure. About to freeze to death."

"What happened?"

"Well, come about Christmastime someone noticed this snow-covered mound in the middle of nowhere and they dug me out still sitting on my horse. They found some wood and built a fire around me. Took 'til spring to thaw me out." He grinned as her startled expression gave way to surprise and then she laughed.

"The cowboys must love to have you spin tall tales around the campfire. That's a really tall one."

He nodded, pleased with having amused her. "Been practicing it for a few months. You're the first one I got to tell it to."

"Best practice a bit more before you tell a bunch of tough cowboys."

They both laughed as their gazes caught like they'd been lassoed in the same coil of rope.

She pulled away first. "So, what really happened?"

"I prayed." He settled back as he recalled the day. "My mother had taught me about God. I believed but didn't think God really cared much about a dirty little boy." He gave a lopsided grin as he realized he used the same words to describe himself as a man as he'd used to describe himself as a boy. "But I didn't have a lot of options so decided to see if God could really hear and answer my prayer."

"And?"

"Maybe it wasn't really a prayer because I think I yelled something like 'God, help me.'"

"What happened?" Her voice was breathless with anticipation and made him feel as if every word he uttered was precious.

"Nothing. It got colder. The snow got worse. I knew I was going to die. I didn't even realize Two Bit had stopped moving. Suddenly, someone grabbed me, dragged me from the saddle and into a warm place." He considered how to tell the rest.

"That man—I'm guessing it was a man—saved your life."

"Yes, he did. He wrapped me in blankets, warmed me slowly. Took care of my fingers and feet so I didn't lose any to frostbite. I was sick for a couple weeks and he fed me like a baby. I owe that man my life."

She sat back. "That's an amazing story. God certainly heard and answered your prayers."

"Yup." He could wait to tell her it was Scout that rescued him, Scout he owed so much to. "I'm still learning to pray, still wondering when it's okay to ask, and still wondering if God is really going to listen to a dirty little boy."

She laughed. "You aren't a dirty little boy. As a child of God you are loved and precious."

Would he ever feel loved and precious? Didn't seem like he would, but her words eased across his mind seeking out crevasses and cracks and pouring in a bit of warm honey.

"It was Scout who found me. I owe him."

Her expression changed so quickly he could hardly believe it. The sunshine went from her eyes, her brows drew together in a harsh vee. "Now you can pay him back." She gave him a good view of her back as she stared out the window.

"Lucy, can't you give him a chance?"

"I gave him plenty. Keep in mind I'm only going because Roy and I need to get away from Smitty."

Gouges dug into his mind and hot water scalded his thoughts. For just a moment he had forgotten he was only a means to an end for her.

Chapter Five

Lucy turned her back to Wade and stared out the window though she saw none of the passing scenery; anger blinded her. Why had she let herself forget why she and Wade and the sleeping Roy were together? It had nothing to do with how Wade made her laugh, how he touched a tender spot in her heart with his description of himself as a dirty little boy. She struggled to ignore the lingering ache as she thought how terrible it was a child should be made to feel that way. And that a man should carry the remnants of such an emotion.

Best she concentrate on the fact she was only an obligation, a means to repay the kindness her father had shown Wade. How ironic her father could stir himself to rescue Wade but not to visit his daughter. So many years she had waited for a visit, clinging to his promise to return within a few weeks.

With fists of steel she punched back her regret and disappointment. She would seek shelter at her father's ranch only because she had no other choice.

But she would not let her father or Wade beguile her into thinking she'd find anything more while there.

Her neck cramped from twisting it so hard to keep her eyes trained out the window and not at the man beside her. There was nothing to see but mile after mile of flat prairie.

She finally turned and studied the other occupants in the semi-full car. A couple of business-looking men sat a few benches away. Both held newspapers in front of them so she got only a glance as they lowered the papers to turn the pages.

At the far end of the car a man slouched low in the seat, his cowboy hat pulled over his face, his booted feet propped on the facing seat. A cowboy sleeping it off, Lucy decided and shifted her gaze to the man and woman across the aisle from the cowboy. They sat prim and proper facing straight ahead. Neither blinked. They could have been made of wax for all the life they showed. Lucy decided they were probably a married couple who'd had a row about something.

Across from the couple sat a woman alone, dressed in black except for a white lace collar making a shy appearance at her neck. Noticing Lucy's gaze the woman gave an overeager smile. Having no wish to engage in conversation with a stranger, Lucy nodded hello and brought her gaze to her hands curled in her lap. If only she'd brought a book but somehow the idea hadn't intruded on her hurried plans. Her only concern had been to escape Smitty. It was still her number-one concern. She'd simply deal with everything else that crossed her path as the necessity arose.

"I think I'll go check on the horses," Wade murmured. "Sweet Queenie put up quite a fuss at being tied up in the car."

Lucy nodded as he slipped away. She looked longingly at Roy curled up and wished she could do the same. She covered a yawn.

"It's a long trip." The black-dressed woman slid closer and leaned forward, eager for conversation. She tittered and ducked her head. "Of course, I suppose that would depend on where you're going."

Lucy had no intention of telling anyone her destination nor where she'd come from. "Where are you headed, ma'am?"

"To Seattle. To see my brother and his wife. Margery—that's his wife—has been ill so they need my help." Her taffeta skirts rustled as she smoothed them. "I never married so I'm grateful when someone offers me a home even if it's only my labor they want." She raised watery blue eyes. "You're so fortunate to have a husband and child."

"I—" Why bother correcting her? If anyone—like

Smitty and his friends—asked if a woman and child were on the train, this woman would only remember a family. "I'm glad they need you."

"My brother is my closest relative. I guess he feels obligated to take care of me."

Lucy ground her teeth together to keep her words from bursting out. She would never let herself be so dependent on a man. There were lots of ways an unmarried woman could take care of herself.

She had a job in the dining room that offered her as much independence as she cared for.

"I'm supposing you are heading back to your home."

Lucy let her suppose whatever she wanted.

"You look like a very happy family. It does my heart good to watch you."

A clatter at the end of the car brought a frightened look to the woman and drew Lucy's eyes in alarm. The cowboy who had lounged in the corner seemed to have fallen off the bench. He now righted himself and fumbled in his pocket. He pulled out a flask and tipped it to his mouth.

"Tsk," the woman in black said. "Public drunkenness is so appalling." She shrank back against the window.

Lucy knew enough to mind her own business and looked out at the passing scenery.

The cowboy staggered to his feet, mumbling to himself. He headed down the aisle, lurching from one bench to the next. He would have to pass Lucy. She kept her gaze pointedly turned away.

He drew closer, still mumbling. He fell into an empty seat, laughed and managed to regain his feet.

She could smell the alcohol on him mixed with rancid sweat. Lucy held her breath and waited for him to safely navigate the next few yards, praying he would pass without incident.

The woman in the opposite seat tsked again, loudly, her disapproval as obvious as a shovel full of dirt.

The cowboy stopped, swaying to stay upright. "Old bat. Dried-up prune."

The woman sucked in air, shocked, no doubt, by the names spewing from the man's mouth.

Lucy didn't allow so much as a twitch to reveal her anxiety.

The train swayed. The cowboy tipped sideways and landed practically in Lucy's lap. She jumped up and perched on the edge of the opposite bench, sharing the space with Roy's feet.

The cowboy peered at her bleary-eyed. His mouth parted in a sloppy grin. "Hey, it's Lucy gal. Whatcha doing here?" He hiccoughed. "Why ain't you serving all them hungry folk back to…to…well, shoot, you know what I mean."

She didn't recognize him. But then hundreds of cowboys ate at the dining room.

The cowboy leaned closer and she shifted back, barely able to keep from pressing her hand to her nose.

"I don't recall seeing you when I got on the train."

Perhaps she could divert him. "Where you headed, mister?"

"Seattle." The word came out so slurred she only guessed that's what he said. He pulled himself as close to upright as he seemed capable. "Say, did you hear some guy was shot in the barn?" His gaze shifted to Roy as if trying to place him.

Lucy prepared to defend the boy but Roy was dead to the world. He hadn't even sighed at the racket.

The black-clad woman made more disapproving noises and the cowboy's eyes narrowed momentarily. Lucy sensed his annoyance with the woman. "I hope they found the killer," the woman said with a sniff.

"Self-defense." The cowboy managed to mangle the word.

"Were you going to check on your horse or perhaps get a drink?"

"Can't remember. Don't care. You never gave me so much as a smile back at the—" His train of thought derailed. He paused, seemed to search his mind for where he meant to go with the conversation. "Now we're traveling companions." He leered in a most disgusting way. "Come and sit by me, Lucy gal." He patted the seat beside him.

When she made no move, he reached for her. The effort tipped him off balance and he fell toward her.

Wade's insides boiled as the drunk fell toward Lucy. His fists clenched as pure, undiluted anger rolled through him. He closed the distance in three strides and grabbed the man by the shoulder, deriving a certain amount of satisfaction from the way he flinched. He hoped there'd be a bruise for weeks to remind the man of the consequence of his inappropriate behavior.

He jerked the man upright, yanked at his belt and rushed him out the door and into the baggage car, dropping him into a mound of hay. "Don't come back. You can sleep it off out here." It required a great deal of self-control to keep from laying a thrashing on him.

He paused several minutes before heading back to the passenger car, waiting for his heart to resume a regular beat.

If Lucy was hurt he might yet use his fists to teach the man a lesson. He didn't expect this was one of the times God would say to turn the other cheek.

His blood still surged through his veins with unusual heat when he reached Lucy's side. "Did he hurt you?"

"I'm all right."

"Glad I got here before he could harm you."

She fixed him with stormy gray eyes. He didn't blame her for being upset. He should never have left her alone, unprotected.

"I could have taken care of myself."

He blinked in surprise that she would object to his help, but then she was used to defending herself against the advances of the many cowboys who took their meals at the dining room. "You don't need to. I'll protect you. I promise you'll always be safe with me." He felt a prick of worry that he couldn't protect her after she returned to Dry Creek if she chose to do so.

"Don't make promises." Her low words carried a note of steel. "I don't trust promises. I learned a long time ago there's no point in looking for a hero. I take care of myself."

He studied her determined expression for a moment. She might as well have painted a sign on her saying "no trespassing." She'd just as effectively created invisible walls.

"I used to think I could manage on my own. This past winter taught me how valuable other people can be."

"I suppose you mean my father."

He sat beside her, ignoring the way she skittered as far away as possible. "Yup."

She gave him a disbelieving look. "Don't expect me to feel the same way."

Lucy obviously did not want to continue the

conversation. She kept her face resolutely toward the window, no doubt drinking in the fascinating scenery—the vast miles of nothing but grass, wheat fields and farms clustered close to the tracks.

He rearranged himself, stretching his legs down the aisle. Even if the drunk cowboy returned, he'd have to climb over Wade to get close to Lucy and that wasn't going to happen. Wade let his head hang down, his chin almost on his chest and allowed sleep to come.

He slept lightly, something a man learned to do on the trail. So he noticed right away when Lucy sighed and straightened to face forward. Guess she got tired of the fascinating scenery. He knew the moment the monotony of the landscape and the clack of the train numbed her brain. Her head fell forward and she followed suit, jolting upright just before she melted to her knees. It was only a matter of time and he waited for the moment, adjusting his height in preparation. It came on angel wings—the peace of sleep. He caught her as she tilted forward and angled her toward him letting her head fall against his shoulder. With a deep sigh of contentment, he settled back and relaxed. She might hate him when she woke but at least she would be able to get a few hours sleep.

An hour or more passed. Roy jerked awake and sat up.

Wade stole a look from under his eyelashes.

Roy's eyes ate up his face as he looked around the

entire car. When he saw no danger he let out a rush of relief. Then another fear seemed to hit him and he scrambled to find the sack holding the lunch they'd picked up.

Wade kept his head down not letting on he was awake. He didn't want to disturb Lucy. Roy however, had no such qualms.

"Lucy," he whispered fiercely. "Wake up."

Lucy sighed and rubbed her cheek along Wade's shoulder.

He buried a smile deep in his heart. It was one of those moments he would hang on his wall of remembrance.

Slept left her in stages. First the nuzzle, then a protesting sigh, followed by shocked stillness as she realized where she was, that she was snuggled up to Wade.

He didn't allow his eyelids to flicker as she bolted upright. Even with his eyes closed he felt her glare sear his skin. When she believed him asleep, she relaxed.

"When did you wake up?" she asked Roy.

"Just now. I'm hungry. Can we eat?"

"We should wait for Wade, don't you think?"

"He might sleep a long time." Roy's voice edged toward panic.

"Roy, you won't starve."

"How do you know? I'm a growing boy, ain't I?"

"Try growing a little patience."

Roy nudged Wade's leg rather sharply. Wade figured he'd done it intentionally, determined to waken him.

"Let him sleep."

Lucy's defense of him was more satisfying than any food he'd eaten.

"How long?"

Lucy sighed. "He's been good enough to drag us along. You might be taking that into consideration."

Wade knew he should let them know he was awake but listening to this conversation was too enjoyable—though being reminded that she'd only come out of desperation nipped at the edges of his enjoyment.

"We're going to your pa?"

Without opening his eyes Wade knew Lucy bristled. "We're going to a ranch farther west. Smitty won't have any way of knowing where we've gone. That's about all we need to know."

"I don't remember my pa."

The boy sure did know how to turn his words into a wistful song.

"Could be your good fortune. Might be he was a scoundrel."

"I wouldn't care. I'd still love him."

Wade tensed, waiting for a reply from Lucy.

"You should be cautious or you'll end up feeling like a kicked dog."

She'd been hurt bad by Scout. Perhaps by some other man, as well. It had left an oozing wound.

"I don't care. I'd still love him." His foot banged against Wade's shin, emphasizing every word. It hurt.

Wade jerked his leg away and opened his eyes. He blinked and yawned as if slowly finding consciousness. "What time is it?"

None of them having a timepiece, they all looked out the window. Roy had his own internal sense of time. "It's way past dinnertime."

"I 'spect it is at that. Wonder where we could get us something to eat?"

Roy rattled the sack. "We got a lunch packed before we got on the train. Did you forget?"

"Why that's right. Is there any left?"

Roy nodded hard. The little towhead needed a haircut. Wade rubbed his neck. He did, too. Maybe when they got to the ranch he'd find a pair of scissors and see what he could do.

"I never touched them. We were waiting for you."

"Well. Let's get at it."

Roy hesitated, halfheartedly offering the sack to Wade.

"You be in charge."

Before Roy could pull anything out, Lucy touched his hand. "Let's say grace." She gave Wade a questioning look as if asking if he would do the praying.

He hesitated. Not because he didn't want to thank the good Lord for food and protection and His many blessings, but because he'd never prayed aloud before others.

Lucy smiled. "Go ahead." She bowed her head.

Wade glanced at Roy. He clutched the bag, his head bowed, his eyes squeezed shut.

Lord God, thank You— He realized he spoke the words inside his head and started over. "Lord God, thank You for Your many blessings and Your love and protection. Amen."

Roy handed Lucy a sandwich, practically tossed one at Wade then unwrapped his own and bit into it. He ate with the gusto only a growing boy or a starving man could bring to the task.

Three thick sandwiches later, Roy slowed down enough to glance out the window. "Are we almost there?"

"It's not far now. Once we get to Minot, we'll change trains."

"How far to the ranch?" Roy persisted, shifting restlessly on the bench.

"Not so far if we go direct, but we won't. Got to hide our tracks, don't you think?"

Roy grew still, his eyes wide as he remembered why they were on this trip. "He won't be able to find us, will he?"

"Not if I have anything to do with it." He'd

do his best to make it impossible to guess where they'd gone.

"We going to live at the ranch?"

"Don't see you have a lot of choice right now. Wouldn't want Smitty to find you, would you?" It wasn't Roy he watched for a reaction. It was Lucy. He'd never given much thought to his future past the next job, the next destination. Now he thought of what it would be like to share it with someone whose eyes went from calm gray to a thunderstorm in a flash, someone who teased him and laughed with him, someone as stubborn as an old oak tree. He decided to test the waters. "'Course, you might all decide to stay."

Lucy's eyes grew brittle. "I prefer to make plans to return to Dry Creek or perhaps a job in some other town where we can forget Smitty and where I depend on no one but myself. Besides, what am I supposed to do on a ranch?"

"You could cook if you want. That'd be a great help."

She tipped her chin upward. "Of course. I intend to pay my way however I can." A sparkle lit her eyes. "Though I know nothing about how to manage on a ranch. You might regret my efforts."

He tried not to imagine her in the kitchen cooking meals and washing the dishes—two jobs he detested. "So long as you don't feed us poison mushrooms I don't think there's much to fear."

"But where does one get supplies? Who provides meat?"

"I will supply the meat and there's a good store of supplies at the ranch. Besides, we aren't beyond civilization. Lark is the nearest town and quite adequate. Anything you need you can get there."

"Good."

At the talk of food, Roy checked the empty lunch bag for crumbs. There were none. It would be way past supper time when they reached the ranch. They'd have to scare up something to eat before then or Roy would surely expire.

The miles clacked away. Heat filled the car relieved only slightly by the ash-laden air coming in the windows. He tried a time or two to make conversation but it required a great deal of effort on his part—Lucy seemed to have sunk into a heat-induced stupor.

The conductor swung through the car. "Minot, next stop, folks."

Lucy looked like someone had thrown water on her best dress with her in it.

He understood her concerns about hiding their tracks but perhaps it was the idea of seeing her father that filled her with apprehension. He couldn't understand it. Scout was a great guy. Hardworking, honest and generous. He'd treated Wade like a son.

He had no more time to mull over the future, nor

wonder about Lucy's past as the train ground to a halt. He grabbed their bags from the overhead shelf.

He led them to a slice of shade on the narrow platform. "Wait here while I get the horses."

Roy dropped the empty sandwich bag and raced after Wade. "How long do we stay here?"

"About an hour."

"Smitty don't know where we are, does he?"

"Don't see how he could." The cowboy still sleeping in the hay might pose a threat. But Lucy had said he was bound for Seattle. "You'll be safe on the ranch," he told the boy as he unloaded their two horses.

"You'll be there, won't you?" Roy asked.

He understood the boy's worry. "I'll be there and so will Mr. Hall and Lucy." He led them down the ramp. Queenie hung her head like an old hound dog. She rolled her eyes to make sure Wade understood how tired she was.

"Why don't Lucy like her pa?"

"Roy, I couldn't say." He glanced in Lucy's direction. She stared down the tracks, her shoulders set in rigid defiance. "Might be wise not to ask her."

"She don't know how lucky she is to have a father."

"That's a fact." But it didn't change how things were.

Roy looked about. "Don't suppose there's a dining room in this town."

"I don't suppose you could be hungry again?"

"A little."

Wade scrubbed his chin, pretended to be in deep thought. They had less than an hour before the next train on the Northern Pacific line. The ranch lay to the north, fifteen miles from the town of Lark along the SOO line but he figured to head west, get off down the line and then ride back. It was circuitous, but meant to be. He hoped it would confuse Smitty if he tried to find them.

"Don't suppose you could miss this one meal?"

Roy hung his head, a perfect match for old Queenie. Maybe the pair had been spending too much time together. Both seemed to have a healthy interest in food. He'd noticed the horse developed the sprightly step of a young colt when he tossed out oats for the horses. He'd had to push her away from Two Bit's share. That gave him an idea. He might be able to put her greedy appetite to good use.

"You ain't got some old biscuits or a can of beans?" Roy persisted. "I like cold beans right from the tin."

Wade guessed he liked anything out of the tin— cold or otherwise. "Fact is I do have two tins. You think Lucy would like cold beans?"

Roy spared Lucy a considering look. "Maybe not. She's a mite fussy about her food." Misery weighed his shoulders down.

Wade decided to stop teasing the boy. "I think we

might find something at that hotel down there." He pointed.

And just like Queenie when she caught the scent of oats, Roy perked right up.

A short time later, Wade felt a lot better having filled up on a generous portion of stew and fresh bread. Lucy barely picked at her food but it wasn't wasted. Roy cleaned up what she didn't eat.

"You sure you don't have a hollow leg?" he asked the boy.

"I'm growing."

Wade laughed. "Roy boy, you keep eating like that and you'll be as big as a house." He glanced at Lucy expecting her to share his amusement but Lucy wore a strained look and gripped her fork so hard her knuckles were white.

After loading the horses onto another train they sat quietly as it pulled from the station. Wade tipped his hat low and tried to be invisible. Lucy sat so stiff and upright that her back didn't touch the bench.

"Relax," he whispered. "No one has noticed us. We're just a family headed west so far as they're concerned."

"I wish I could relax," she whispered back. "But I feel like I'm stuck between a rock and...." She shrugged and didn't finish.

He didn't need her to.

Twenty minutes later they slipped off the train and gathered the horses. Then headed south away from the ranch, Queenie acting put upon because she was expected to move faster than a caterpillar without legs. Wade paused and opened the bag of oats. He put a layer in his hat and held it out. Sure enough, sad, worn-out Queenie perked her ears and trotted toward him. He gave his hat to Roy. "Keep shaking it but don't let her reach it."

"I see you aren't above a little trickery." Lucy's words were drummed out of her by Queenie's rough trot.

"I like to think I'm smarter than an animal." They made a few miles. He hated to keep Lucy at that pace. She'd be beat to pieces by the time they got to the ranch. But if he slowed, the horse would grab the oats. He urged Two Bit to a lope. Queenie whinnied a protest then settled back into her plodding walk. "I guess she's not up for a challenge."

"She can't run that fast." Roy defended his pet.

The title of pet suited her better than that of saddlehorse. They managed a few more erratic miles with Queenie dashing for the oats if he allowed Two Bit to slow, and then slowing to a crawl if Two Bit sped up.

"Remind Queenie of the oats."

Roy shook the hat. "Come on, Queenie. Here's something to eat."

Wade could almost hear Lucy's teeth rattle as Queenie trotted toward the treat. He tensed his jaw. He couldn't stand to watch Lucy shook up like that.

"Watch the oats." He jumped from the saddle and grabbed Queenie's reins before she could knock Roy off Two Bit's back. "We're going to change places," he told Lucy and reached up for her.

She tried to swing off the saddle but her skirts caught and she tumbled into his arms. He felt her galloping heartbeat thud through her body, no doubt jolted into such a pace by Queenie's rough gait. She clutched her arms around his neck and hung on like she'd found home sweet home. He held her tight both to calm her shudders and to still the blessed lurch of pleasure at the weight of her in his grasp; the alarming, unfamiliar way his heart swelled against his ribs as if it were reaching toward *her* heart to calm it. To hold it. To cherish it.

What had been in that stew? Whatever strange ingredient, it certainly had affected his ability to think straight. He swung Lucy toward Two Bit. "You ride my horse. Otherwise, I can see us riding all night to get a few miles."

She scrambled into the saddle. Roy clung to her waist. Wade allowed himself a quick glance, noting the pink in Lucy's cheeks. He'd embarrassed her and chewed on the thought a moment. He regretted making her uncomfortable, but decided if he said anything he'd further discomfort them both. Grinding down on his molars in disgust at himself and his stupid reaction, he swung onto Queenie's back. "Keep the oats where she can see them." He faced straight ahead. "Keep a good pace. Whatever's comfortable. We'll keep up."

"I don't know where I'm going."

Her words blazed across his brain. He didn't know where he was going either. "Just head down the trail. Two Bit knows the way." He'd gotten all twisted up with thoughts of sweet little Lucy—a woman who said time and time again she had no use for a man, no faith in promises and had made it clear she would not trust another.

But none of that mattered more than a heap of straw. He only wanted to take her to Scout before the man died. He owed him that much.

Chapter Six

Throughout the train ride and as they left behind the tracks to wander from one direction to another, Lucy worried how she'd face meeting her father again. Now, after what seemed like hours on horseback, her muscles cried out for relief and she no longer cared who or what waited for them at the end of the trail. All she wanted was to get out of this saddle and find a soft place to stretch out and give her body a chance to relax.

Roy had long ago stuck the hat of oats between them and leaned his head against her back. She wouldn't wonder if he'd fallen asleep.

Wade fought Queenie every step of the way.

Lucy turned to check on their progress. The old horse amazed her. Where did she get the energy to keep fighting? Talk about stubborn. Maybe she was part mule.

Wade noticed her watching and widened his mouth in a gesture as much grimace as smile. He had the look of a man pushed way beyond his level of patience. And she grinned, just a tiny bit pleased at his struggle. Somehow it felt like justice to see him having to cope with a stubborn animal and his frustration drained some of hers.

Roy slumped to one side.

She reached back and steadied him. "Stay awake or you'll fall off."

He mumbled something and righted himself.

Darkness crept in, gray and gentle. Pink tinted the western sky and ribbons of purple, orange and red crossed it, too. Then the gray deepened. Lucy struggled to keep her eyes open and prayed they would arrive soon, before she and Roy both fell off and decided to spend the night sleeping on the prairie.

Wade took the reins from her, and she realized they'd stopped moving.

"We're here." He lifted Roy from the horse and put him on the ground where he crumpled into a ball, asleep.

"Thank God." Gratitude rounded her words as much as fatigue. "But where exactly is *here?*"

"The ranch." He offered his hand to help her down.

She hesitated. Her heart, which moments before had slowed to sleep mode, kicked into a gallop as she remembered falling into his arms a short time after they started this torturous ride. She'd embarrassed them both with the way she clung to him even though it was only because she shook clear through from riding Queenie. That was her excuse and she didn't intend to allow any other reason to intrude. But the idea of a repeat performance both tempted and frightened her.

"This is the ranch?" She strained to see anything in the darkness, using the time to get her feelings under control. "I don't see anything."

"We're at the corrals. There's a low barn to your right."

She followed the line of wooden fence to a building. "I see it."

"You can't see the house in the dark, but it's over there." He pointed to the left then reached for her again.

She allowed him to take her hand and slowly eased down, determined she would not throw herself into his arms this time.

Her legs buckled as they took her weight and she clung to his hand as longing surged up her throat. Why had she thought she didn't want to find security against his solid chest?

Because she did not, would not, could not ever let herself pin her hopes and dreams on a man. Nor could she afford to forget that he wanted her here for only one reason—his obligation to Scout. She forced steel into her legs and released his hand. "Thank you."

"Wait with Roy while I turn the horses into the corral." His voice sounded faintly amused with just a pinch of regret, as if he'd read her thoughts.

She leaned against the fence. She would have liked to curl up beside Roy but knew if she did, she would never be able to get up and make the journey to the house. Peering into the darkness, she made out the faint shape of a building beneath the limbs of a big tree. Was it the house? But wouldn't the house have a light burning?

She turned her gaze away and tried to tear her thoughts from what lay ahead. In a few minutes she would come face-to-face with the father she'd never been able to count on. The entire long weary day she'd dreaded this moment, wondered what she'd say. *Lord, hold me up through this. Let me not be disappointed again.*

"Are you ready?" Wade asked.

She hadn't heard him and jumped. "Yes." *No.* How could she be ready for something she didn't want and had promised to never again put herself through? She used to eagerly run to the window when someone entered the yard, wondering if her papa had come. She'd stood at the same window, washing it with her tears when he left. As he always did. Leaving behind a little girl who wanted so much for her papa to notice her enough to do more than say hello.

Her heart filled with angry determination. She would not let him hurt her again.

Wade scooped Roy into his arms and she followed him across the yard toward the darkened building she'd studied.

A low growl stopped her in her tracks. The skin on the back of her neck tingled. "What's that?" she croaked.

"It's Bear," Wade said. "He's just warning us in case we're up to some mischief."

"Bear?" That's all she needed. A pet bear. Of course, he hadn't said it was a pet. She began to back up.

"He won't hurt you unless—"

"I don't want to know what's *unless*." Her whisper scratched from her throat.

Wade's boots echoed on wood. She guessed he had reached the steps but she didn't join him. A few minutes ago, she'd been so tired she could barely walk, but now she had the urge to run into the dark. Only uncertainty of what lay out there stopped her.

"Hey, Hunter. It's me, Wade. Call off your dog."

Wade's loud voice jerked across Lucy's tense nerves, and she pressed her hands to her chest as she tried to calm her heart.

Dog? Was Bear a dog? Something creaked. A door opening?

"That you, Wade?"

"Yes. Give us some light, man."

A match flared. The smell of sulfur filled the air. Then a lamp glowed yellow revealing a wizened, bewhiskered man and a hairy dog at his side almost as tall as the man. The dog stood with his hackles raised and white fangs bared.

Lucy's heart kicked against her palm. She backed up several more steps, stumbled and righted herself.

"Yup. It's you all right. Bear, settle down."

The dog stopped growling.

The fact did nothing to ease Lucy's fears.

"I got company," Wade said. "Scout's daughter and a young lad who refuses to wake up."

"Come in the house. I want to get back to me bed."

Wade headed for the door. "Come on, Lucy. We're home." He glanced over his shoulder. "What are you doing way back there?"

She didn't spare him a look, couldn't take her eyes off that animal, certain the moment she did it would rumble from the house and attack her. She didn't want Wade to realize her fear and tried to make her feet move, tried to force a calm word from her throat. All she managed was a squeak.

"You afraid of Bear?" His voice said it all. Amazement, surprise, and a generous dollop of pity.

But she still couldn't make her feet move.

"Hunter, take the boy." The man set the lamp on a stand and Wade shifted Roy's weight to his arms then strode back to Lucy. "Come on. I'll protect you."

She didn't miss the humor lacing his words.

Normally she would have resented him suggesting she needed protecting, but somehow her pride had deflated at the sight of the large dog.

Wade wrapped an arm around her shoulders and led her to the step. Hunter and his dog moved aside to let them pass.

She swallowed hard as they made it safely into the house and tried not to think of the dog only inches from her. An impossible task when she could smell him with every tight breath. Surely, he wasn't allowed to sleep indoors.

Warmth crept up her throat as she realized she stood pressed to Wade's side and she eased away, though not too far. He provided her only protection if the dog lurched at her.

"How's Scout?" Wade kept his voice low.

Roy mumbled and squirmed. Hunter set him on his feet. The boy practically melted to the floor then found the door frame and propped himself against it.

"Scout's still hanging on. Sleeping now, of course. Don't think you want to disturb him, do ya?"

Wade shook his head. "Of course not. Besides, we're all about ready for some shut-eye ourselves."

Lucy could make out little of the house—just enough to see they stood in a kitchen of sorts with a cookstove and a few cupboards. A round table across the room was piled high with unidentifiable objects.

Past the table she made out a doorway but couldn't tell what lay beyond.

"Scout still in the living room?"

"Yup."

"You're sleeping in the loft?"

"Yup. Plenty of room for ya'll."

Lucy made out a ladder beside the table, leading to an area with a half wall. She stared at it. Was she expected to sleep there with the men?

Wade touched her elbow. "I have a place for you. Come."

She hesitated. "What about Roy?"

"I'll take care of him."

She still didn't move, concerned for the boy. But her fears subsided as she realized Wade had done a fine job of seeing to them so far. She allowed him to lead her across the room.

He lit another lamp and led her to a door she hadn't noticed beyond the stove. She stepped into a narrow room, just wide enough for a cot with an open cupboard crammed in at the foot of the bed. Not that she had anything to put into it. Her belongings fit into the rather small bag that Wade dropped on the floor.

The place smelled of flour and coffee.

Wade lit a lantern by the door where he hovered. "It used to be the pantry but I figured if you came, you'd need a place of your own. This is it. Good night." He gave her a short nod then closed the door with haste.

Through the dim light, Lucy took in the bed covered with a Hudson Bay blanket. A green blind covered the one narrow window. Lucy rubbed her palms up and down her arms trying to drive away a chill that went deep into her soul and would not be relieved by warming her skin. Her father apparently slept a few feet away, separated by mere lathe and plaster walls. She would not be able to avoid seeing him within the next few hours. The idea caught at her heart, whipping it into a frenzy not unlike her reaction to the big dog. This time she could not find strength in Wade's touch.

Her heart gave a vicious lurch against her ribs as she thought how she'd practically glued herself to Wade's side. So much for proving she needed no one.

Determination gave momentum to her limbs. She needed no one. She would face whatever this decision required of her and she would come out unscathed from it. Even if she had to nail boards over her thoughts and emotions.

Having established the ground rules for her stay here, she checked the door to make sure it was firmly closed, blew out the lamp, then climbed into bed where she lay shivering under the covers even though the room was warm.

Lucy struggled from sleep as a strange noise woke her. The room was already brightly lit. A fly buzzed against the window. She turned to squint at the window and sat bolt upright when she saw it now went from ceiling to elbow height. Then she remembered. She wasn't in her little room in Dry Creek. She was at her father's ranch.

Falling back onto the cot, she closed her eyes and groaned. Not much chance she could avoid seeing him today.

She listened to the clack clack of a dog's nails as it crossed the floor. The outer door opened and a voice said, "Out."

"Lucy," Roy called.

"Let her sleep. She was pretty tired."

Hearing Wade's voice, she grinned. So, he thought to let her sleep, did he? The idea made her feel a little spoiled, as if she deserved to be given special regard.

"I'm awfully hungry."

Her grin grew wider. Roy was always hungry.

"Who's going to make breakfast?"

"I can cook," Wade answered.

"Like Miss Hettie?"

"'Fraid not."

"Then maybe we should wake Lucy up so she can cook."

Then she remembered that she'd agreed to cook while she was staying at the ranch. Breakfast depended on her. Might as well get up and face the day, her responsibilities and—when he could no longer be avoided—her father.

She pulled on her clothes, ignoring the way her legs ached from so many hours on horseback. She smoothed her hair. As soon as possible, she would slip out to the facilities. She paused at the door, not sure how to deal with what lay on the other side.

Lord God, guide me. Give me strength. Her world righted as she centered her thoughts on God's love and care. She'd learned to trust Him. Being here didn't change that.

The door opened quietly, not alerting any of the others to her presence. Roy sat at the table examining the contents of used cups as if hoping to find sustenance, pushing them aside with a deep sigh when they yielded none. Wade's attention was on filling a kettle from a bucket of water.

Hunter was missing as was, thankfully, his huge dog.

"How long before she wakes up?" Roy sounded desperate.

"I'm awake."

Wade spun around to face her.

She'd cleaned up as best she could. She normally pinned her hair into a roll but discovered most of her pins had disappeared so she'd braided it into a long plait that hung down her back.

Wade's gaze lingered on her hair and his eyes widened, making her blush. Did he think her hair inappropriate? She tilted her chin slightly. She had done the best she could. No one could expect more.

Then he met her eyes, correctly reading the challenge in them. He grinned. "Morning, Lucy. You look refreshed so I'm guessing you slept well. Last night you seemed a little—" His grin widened and she had the sneaky suspicion he recalled her seeking shelter at his side. "You seemed a little shaky."

"It was a long day." She wouldn't think of that incident or the way her heart had done a slow swoop when she woke on the train with her face pressed to his shoulder. She had feigned sleep several seconds as she'd examined her reaction. He'd felt so solid. So comforting.

She shifted her thoughts back to reality. They were here only to hide from Smitty. Only to fulfill what Wade considered to be an obligation to her father. In that equation there bode no room for silly weaknesses. Not that she would allow them in any case. Last night had been an exception.

She turned to Roy, his eyes widening as he silently pleaded for food. Only she couldn't run into the kitchen and beg a plateful from Hettie. She'd have to find the makings and cook the food before any of them could eat. "Show me where you keep your supplies and I'll start breakfast before Roy fades away to a shadow."

Wade chuckled. "He's been on the verge for several minutes." He pointed to a door in the floor by the table. "Our supplies are in the cellar. There's lots of things like oatmeal, flour, cornmeal—"

"Can you make corn bread?" Roy asked with such eagerness Lucy glanced at Wade and they both laughed.

She ducked away from the mirth in Wade's eyes, eyes that seemed to offer her so many things. She ground down on her back teeth. She knew the pain and futility of waiting for anyone else to provide what she needed. She found her belonging in God alone and His love. How could she be forgetting her hard-won lessons when her father lay only a few feet away?

Her gaze slid toward the next room.

Wade misinterpreted the action. "I suppose you're anxious to see Scout?"

She half shook her head but until she dealt with this, it would hang over her head like a doomsday ball ready to drop. "Is he awake?"

"Yup. I spoke to him a few minutes ago. He'll be anxious to see you."

Lucy noticed Wade didn't say her father had actually *said* he was anxious to see her. Likely Wade simply assumed it. "How is he?" She'd heard him cough several times during the night and tried not to feel anything but normal concern—one human for another.

"He's weak but—"

She nodded, her gaze stuck at the doorway, her

mouth wooden so she couldn't talk. This shouldn't be a big deal. She'd long ago mentally said goodbye, yet...

Hope and regret, dreams and reality clashed so violently, she shuddered.

Again Wade misinterpreted her action. "Don't worry. He's well enough to see you. Come." He stepped toward the doorway.

Her legs refused to move as she remembered the many times she'd run to other doors, in other houses, anxious for a glimpse of her father. The few times he came, it had been for fleeting visits. His whole visit seemed to revolve around fixing things for Mama. Lucy had hovered in the background aching for recognition, a kind word, anything. The most he ever gave was an awkward pat to her head and perhaps a piece of penny candy.

His leaving had left her wallowing in regret and denial. He'd be back. He'd said he would and she'd believed him and believed that when he returned he'd spend time with her. Only he never came back when he said he would. Sometimes it was months, even years. She forced that memory to the forefront. This was a man who made promises but didn't keep them, who didn't see how deep her need had been for a real father.

Wade waited expectantly, his expression eager.

Wade's only reason for bringing her, for taking care of her and Roy was to meet his own sense of obligation. She pushed that realization to the front, too.

Stiffening her resolve, she followed Wade into the other room, stopping just past the door to look around. A fireplace dominated a long wall in the untidy room. Chairs and a writing table stood at the far end. At last, when there was no more option, she let her gaze slide to the sofa at the far end of the room where someone lay covered by a gray woolen blanket.

"Hello, Lucy. I see you made it." Her father's voice set off familiar memories. He sounded the same. She expected he was the same in other respects, too.

"Hello, Father." Seems she should be able to think of something more to say but only accusations and questions came to mind and she had no intention of voicing them.

To save them both further discomfort, Lucy shifted her gaze to Wade. He watched her as if hoping for more from her, wondering at the stiffness between her and Scout. But Wade couldn't begin to understand how it felt to have a father who had never managed to give her more than a passing glance during his fleeting visits.

Wade and Roy were both orphans. They knew why their fathers didn't have a role in their lives.

Her father simply chose not to be part of hers.

Roy sidled into the room.

"Who is this young fella?" Scout asked.

Lucy decided his voice was weaker than she remembered. He certainly looked smaller under the covers. Guess being sick could do that to a man. He was paler, too. Last time she'd seen him she'd thought he looked especially handsome with his bronzed skin.

Wade answered Scout's question. "This is Roy. A friend of Lucy's."

"Glad to have you join us, Roy," her father said.

He hadn't said he was glad to see Lucy nor sounded half as welcoming. Rather than think further along that line, she forced herself to look out the window and note the bright sky, the rolling prairie.

After another awkward moment she said, "I suppose I better start breakfast."

That got Roy's attention and he raced back to the kitchen to stand staring at the cellar trapdoor. "Can I go down?"

Wade laughed and explained to Scout, "Roy is a growing boy who seems to need to eat all the time."

Scout grinned. "Best see to it then." He coughed.

Lucy waited, hoping for more, but Scout lay back against the pillows and closed his eyes. She ground around on her heels and followed Wade back to the kitchen. Anger at herself as much as at anyone else churned through her.

"I guess we're safe from Smitty for now. For that

I should be grateful." Her words came out clipped as bullets.

Caution filled his eyes. "You sound anything but."

"I am. Now where's the food?"

He studied her a moment then lifted the trapdoor. "Let's have a look."

Roy scampered down. Wade followed and waited at the bottom of the ladder to help Lucy. She ignored him and made her own way.

The storeroom was cool. Lots of canned and dry goods but no fresh produce. No eggs. Only tinned milk. She could see cooking might be a challenge.

"I think we'll settle for griddle cakes this morning. Maybe some tinned peaches." She let Roy carry the items up to the kitchen.

As she mixed the batter hoping it would be edible without an egg, Roy watched her every move. From the meals he'd taken at the dining room she knew Wade liked coffee so she made a pot.

Hunter stepped inside, his dog waiting on the step. Good place for a dog. Even from there, she could smell the animal. "Now you all are back, I'se heading back to my place."

"You're welcome to stay for breakfast," Wade said.

But the man shook his head. "Got to go."

"Thanks for staying with Scout."

Relief gusted from Lucy's lungs as the man stomped off, the huge dog at his side.

She cleaned soiled dishes from the table, cleared it of assorted tools and papers and scrubbed it until it was fit to eat off. Then she served the griddle cakes, peaches and for Wade, coffee.

When she stood back waiting for them to eat, Wade pulled out a third chair. "You ain't waiting tables here. Sit down with us and eat."

For a moment she wanted to refuse. It was easier to keep a protective barrier around herself if she kept the lines clearly drawn. She was here seeking protection and paying her keep by cooking. Sitting at the table, sharing the meal, blurred the lines.

"We aren't going to eat while you stand there."

At Wade's announcement, Roy swallowed so hard she almost laughed.

"Come on, Lucy. Ain't you always saying we should remember to act like family when we get the chance?"

"Roy, someday I'm going to teach you to remember my remarks when it's for your enlightenment, not mine."

He looked offended. "Well, you did say it, didn't you?"

"I did, but I meant—" What did it matter that she had been trying to teach him how normal people functioned?

Her gaze went unbidden to the living room door. Did she take food to her father or...

Wade touched the back of her hand, sending tingles through her veins. It was about all she could do not to turn her palm to his and hang on for dear life. Instead, she jerked away telling herself she didn't care that his eyes narrowed and hoarded a look of pain.

"He's sleeping," Wade said. "You can take him something later. In the meantime, you might as well enjoy breakfast with us."

Compared to sharing the meal with her father— trying to make conversation when they had nothing to connect them except her mother—Wade's invitation seemed rather pleasant. "Very well." She got herself a plate and silverware and sat in the chair Wade pulled out.

"Thank you. This is better. Shall I say grace?"

She'd noticed his hesitation on the train, guessed praying out loud was something new for him so his offer diffused her annoyance, replacing it with something akin to pleasure.

The three of them bowed their heads as Wade said a simple grace, then Roy attacked the food.

Wade drained his cup but when Lucy started to get up to refill it, he pressed his hand to her shoulder. "I can do it. You enjoy your breakfast." He poured a second cup of coffee and returned to the table.

She ducked her head to hide her hot cheeks. His consideration did something warm and fuzzy to her.

For a moment she could forget her father lay in the other room—the only reason Wade cared whether or not she was here.

Chapter Seven

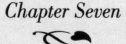

The stove belched out heat. The kitchen grew impossibly warm even though a breeze blew through the open door and windows. Lucy washed the breakfast dishes plus others she'd gathered up around the room. Wade had told her Scout would call when he woke up. So far he hadn't; though she'd heard him cough several times.

And she was grateful for the reprieve. Somehow, she had to find a way to keep her boundaries firmly fixed. Not that it was as hard with her father as it seemed to be with Wade.

She stared out the window. Wade and Roy had left after breakfast to tend to chores. She'd seen them a couple of times carrying things from one spot to another. Each time her heart did a swoop and then climbed like a bird set free to soar the winds. It had taken a firm hand to clip her heart's wings.

When would she ever learn to stop aching after attention and acknowledgment? She'd diverted her futile longings from her father only, apparently, to settle them on Wade.

God help me be wise. I need no one but You. You are my all in all.

"Hunter? Are you there?" Her father's voice came from the other room, ending on a cough.

She had to face him.

Gathering up her strength, remembering her prayer for wisdom, she went to the living room. "Hunter has gone home. I'm here. Can I get you something to eat?"

"What do you have?"

She ignored the feeling that she should whip out an order book and pencil to write down his selection. "Griddle cakes and peaches. Would you like coffee?"

"Sounds fine." He barely looked at her.

She took the water glass from the table at his side and returned to the kitchen. She could do this. It was no different than the work she'd done back at the Dry Creek dining room. Take orders, dish up food, refill cups.

Only back there it had been fun.

So, why not make this fun? Just because it was her father and he treated her like she was invisible didn't mean she had to act any differently than if he was a rowdy cowboy.

She turned her attention to the stove to set the griddle over the heat. Wisps of smoke came from the fat burning off it. The fire snapped.

She spooned batter to the hot griddle and smiled. At first it felt forced. Then she nodded. "Lucy gal here to serve you, sir." She tried a little laugh and swayed her hips as if avoiding an overeager cowboy. "Coffee coming up." She giggled as she imagined Harry hovering in the background ready to straighten out her father.

Wade stood a few feet from the open doorway, staring as he watched Lucy sway and talk to herself. Something about bringing coffee. He settled back on his heels, enjoying her smile and laugh. Her reaction to her father this morning had baffled him. The pair seemed as strained as strangers forced together in tight quarters. Of course he knew they hadn't seen each other in some time. But to see her relaxed now and enjoying herself like the first time he'd seen her eased his concerns. Her tautness was gone.

He'd done the right thing bringing her here. Right for Scout and right for her. Right for him, too? He couldn't say just yet but he sure did like to see her dancing about the kitchen. "Nice to see you happy."

She jumped a good eight inches and grabbed at her chest. Her expression lost all joy. "You ought to know better than to sneak up on people and scare them."

"I just wanted a drink."

"How long were you standing there?" Her eyes narrowed with suspicion. "You been spying?"

He felt his eyes crinkle, knew they gave away the truth, not only that he'd seen but enjoyed watching her. "Nice dance."

She sniffed.

For a moment he thought she was going to blast him with anger, then the storm in her eyes fled before the sunshine of her smile and she giggled. "I was practicing."

"Yeah? For what?"

She turned her attention to flipping the griddle cakes but not before he saw how she sobered. He wondered at the cause.

Then she faced him, her jaw set determinedly. "To wait on my father."

"Huh?" That made not one speck of sense. Shouldn't she be happy to do so? Then he knew he could no longer deny the fact she wasn't here because of any affection for her father. She'd only come with him to escape Smitty. The tension in his jaw grew so fierce he figured it might take a pry bar to force it open. No reason he should think how much he'd like for her to stay. He just wished he could figure out why Lucy was so unforgiving toward her father.

She must have sensed his questions coming

because she shrugged. "I'm just being silly. What's the harm in that?"

"Nothing. I guess." Still, her words didn't sit quite right with him. As if she had to practice being nice to Scout. Didn't make sense. But then not much about her feelings for her father did.

She flipped the cakes to a plate, spooned on peaches, filled a cup with coffee and stood facing the living room but making no move in that direction. Then she swung her head, sending her long plait dancing and it seemed she forced a smile to her lips. "Want to grab a coffee for yourself and bring it along?"

He'd only intended to have a cup of cold water but he couldn't resist her invitation. Besides, he wanted to see the two of them together again. He filled a cup and followed her.

Scout sat up on the couch with a piece of wood across his lap to use as a tray. He must have been hungry because he didn't even glance up as Lucy put the food before him. He ate slowly, but he ate it all.

That was good. Last time Wade had been there to take food to Scout he had turned away from it. Of course, his cooking didn't hold a candle to Lucy's.

Yes, siree, having Lucy here was going to be good for Scout.

Scout turned his attention to his coffee. "How are the cows?" he asked Wade.

"Haven't had a chance to ride out and check them yet."

"Didn't you bring a boy with you? Where is he?"

"Out exploring."

Scout grinned. "Bet he'll like the open spaces as much as we do." The man's gaze skittered past Lucy without pausing.

Wade resisted an urge to sigh. Of course, it would take time for both Scout and Lucy to feel relaxed around each other. Likely they'd have lots of time because while Smitty roamed free there wasn't any place much safer than right here.

Scout finished and pushed his dishes aside.

Lucy gathered them up and headed for the kitchen.

Neither daughter nor father had spoken a word to each other.

As Lucy dumped the dishes into the dishpan, Wade thought he heard her mutter, "You're welcome."

How strange. Scout hadn't even thanked her for breakfast.

This pair had a long way to go.

He followed Lucy back to the kitchen and watched her washing dishes, her thick braid following every movement of her hands. "I'm sure he's grateful even though he didn't say so."

She glanced over her shoulder.

Relief eased his chest muscles when he saw that she smiled.

"No, you're grateful. But it doesn't matter. I've had lots of experience waiting on customers."

So, that's what she'd been doing while he'd

watched through the open door—practicing waiting on customers. But why should she think it was her role with her father? The idea stung clear through to his cowboy boots. It would take time. That was all, he assured himself, ignoring the way he ached to pull her close and tell her she was so much more than a serving girl.

"Thanks for the coffee." He strode across the yard with the hurry of a man fleeing the hounds of a posse. Only in his case it was the barking of his own confused thoughts that chased him. He'd more than half fallen in love with Lucy before they left Dry Creek. On the trip to the ranch, he'd come dangerously close to leaving the halfway mark in the dust even though he knew how foolish it was. But seeing Lucy with her golden-brown braid dangling down her back swinging with every movement, seeing her in the house and remembering the pleasure of sitting at a meal she'd prepared threatened his last grasp on sensibility. There was no point in getting any foolish thought in his head—not when she viewed him with the same mistrust she eyeballed Scout with. As if just by being a man, he could not be trusted.

Seems she'd have to solve some problems with her pa before she'd see him as anything more than a man to avoid.

He reached the corrals and paused to study the surrounding landscape. *God, seems I'm always asking for favors 'cause here I am with another one. Could*

You please change Lucy's mind about men in general but especially about Scout…and maybe about me?

Lucy closed her eyes as anger threatened to fuel a burst of hurtful words. She knew better than to expect anything different from her father. For years she'd protected herself from his hurtful behavior by not seeing him or corresponding with him. But all that had been changed by Smitty. She'd been able to find no other option but to come here. Which didn't mean she had to let the past hurt her even though it lay on the sofa in the other room, a very real presence.

She cleaned up the last of the dishes and tried to bring some sort of harmony to her thoughts but they were a tangle of hope and despair regarding her father, worry over her and Roy's safety, and anticipation over Wade. She shook her head at her foolishness. Anticipation of what? It wasn't like he wanted her here for any reason except her father's kindness to him. Besides, she reminded herself firmly, she didn't intend to place her happiness on the shoulders of anyone apart from herself and her assurance of God's love.

That thought righted her instantly. She'd learned to trust God's love and it had proved more than adequate.

That dealt with, it was time to earn her keep.

She opened the cupboard door and groaned. The dishes inside were spotted as if they'd had no more than a passing acquaintance with hot water. She scraped filth off the shelves with her fingernail. Her work was cut out for her.

The kitchen was hot enough to bake fluffy biscuits, too hot to work in. She went out to the wide step that ran the length of the cabin. A lean-to roof sheltered it and the breeze swept around the walls of the house. It was reasonably cool here and a bench stood close to the kitchen door. She carried the dishpan outside and washed dishes for an hour, changing the water twice. Before she returned them to the cupboard, she scrubbed it with a brush she found tucked away unused. That done, she attacked the windows and floor.

"Could I have fresh water?" Scout called.

She pushed to her feet, wiped her brow on the towel and filled a shining clean cup.

He struggled up on one elbow as he took the cup and drained the contents then handed it back to her. "Where's Wade and that young fella?"

Not a word of acknowledgment. As it had always been. Why? What had she done wrong? Where had she failed? She fought back the questions. She would ask them no more—not of herself and never of her father. That was the past. She cared only about the future. As soon as it was safe she would return to Dry Creek or move on to something new. She knew how to work. She intended to be self-sufficient.

"Last time I saw them they were out nailing a plank on a fence."

"Good man, Wade is. Proved himself a number of times this past winter. Did he tell you how I found him in a snowstorm?"

She nodded. Realized he wasn't looking at her. As if it somehow hurt him to even see her. "Yes, he told me."

"'Spect they'll be in for dinner soon. You got something ready?"

Lord, give me patience. Protect my heart.

"I'll get right at it." She spun around and hurried back to the kitchen where she stood gasping for air and realized she'd held her breath the whole time she was in the other room.

Why did she still let her father affect her so?

Suddenly, she realized if she didn't hurry, Wade and Roy would be stuck eating who knows what— probably cold tinned beans, which gave her an idea for dinner. She whipped up a huge batch of corn bread, hoping it would be moist without the benefit of eggs and stuck it in the oven. If there were leftovers she could fry them for supper. She opened several tins of beans and put them to heat. If only she had a few more supplies—like vegetables and fruit. Dessert would round out the meal enough to fill a hungry man. But what could she make? She poked through the supplies in the cellar, found some hard raisins. She covered them with boiling water and set them to soak. Thankfully, there was a good supply of flour. She mixed up sweet dumplings and dropped them in the boiling raisin mixture. They would be ready before dinner was over.

A few minutes later she had the table set amidst a sparkling clean kitchen. When she heard boots on the wooden porch floor, she took a deep breath. Preparing the meal had been fun. She'd enjoyed playing house. In her pretense, she'd allowed a few thoughts as to how Wade would be pleased.

Enough. She didn't need his approval or recognition any more than she needed or expected her father's. She'd long ago outgrown such childish notions. She was a strong woman on her own. God loved her and that was all she needed. She had a job—or at least had had one. If she couldn't return to Dry Creek she would find work elsewhere. She would be independent.

The way Wade always said please and thank-you brought him to mind.

But she knew she was only a thank-you to Scout for rescuing him.

Before she could firmly rearrange her thoughts, Wade strode through the door. She hoped the embarrassment tightening her cheeks wouldn't show.

Wade stopped and looked around. A smile started on his lips, flashed to his eyes and landed with a gentle plop in the middle of her heart.

So much for not taking his acknowledgment personally.

"You've cleaned the place. Looks good. I had no idea the floor was so brown."

She was pleased at his praise despite all the silent admonitions she'd barely finished delivering. All that foolishness about not caring.

"My mother taught me well." And her father had taught her even more thoroughly the futility of letting what someone thought matter.

Roy skidded in behind Wade. Dirt freckled his face. He'd found an old gray cap somewhere and it sat at a jaunty angle, his straw-colored hair poking out six ways to Sunday. He fair bubbled with excitement. "You should see all the lumber. Stacks of it. Wade says Scout plans to build a new barn. Wade is going to stay and help do it. I helped stake out where the new barn is going."

It was great to see Roy being included in the work and being under the leadership of someone like Wade. She darted a glance at Wade, caught him studying her, a pensive look in his eyes. She held his gaze a moment, wondering at how he searched past the surface.

What did he hope to see? To discover?

There were no deep dark secrets in her life. At least none that she cared to share.

She shifted her attention back to Roy. "My ma

would scrub your skin raw if she saw that dirty face."

Roy gave her a look full of wariness as if he feared she would do the same.

She laughed. "Good thing for you I'm not so inclined. I'll let you do your own scouring." She pointed to the washbasin. Only when he ducked to splash water over his face did she return her gaze to Wade. He still wore that probing look that sent nervous tremors skittering one way and then the other across her chest.

"I fear I haven't lived up to my training. Ma wouldn't have stopped cleaning until every spider had packed its bag and headed north to Alaska."

"Your ma didn't tolerate dirt well." Her father's voice from the living room ended on a cough. But she'd detected his note of annoyance.

All the enjoyment she'd gotten from Wade noticing her work instantly evaporated. Ma had been far too complacent about Scout's empty promises. Lucy told her time and again to forget him and accept the interest of one of the many men who wanted to call on her—good, decent, churchgoing men. But Ma always said Pa had promised to marry her and she had agreed. She wouldn't back out on her word. "Ma didn't tolerate a dirty house but she was maybe too tolerant of people."

Her father didn't answer. How could he? There was no excuse, no defense for getting a woman with child out of wedlock and then not marrying her. It had taken Lucy a long time to get over the stigma associated with that. In fact, she'd had to move away from her hometown, though once Ma died that was no hardship. In Dry Creek, where no one knew her shameful past, she'd found acceptance. She'd discovered her own strength, and through letting God's love heal her past, her own worth.

She wouldn't let having to find shelter at her father's ranch rob her of that.

Wade's glance shifted. Lucy felt his wariness and maybe even a touch of reproach.

It stung that he'd witnessed this exchange between her father and herself. No doubt she sounded like a mean-spirited daughter. How little he knew of the situation. Mentally, she shrugged. She was here to hide from Smitty and had agreed to housekeeping duties while they remained. How difficult could it be for all of them to do their own thing without intruding into each other's lives?

She flashed Wade a grin, determined to keep things rolling along on the clear path set before her. "Well, cowboy, I hope you aren't fussy about your food. I did the best I could but I gotta say your pantry isn't as well-stocked as Hettie's. Could be she takes her cooking a little more seriously than you do, among other things." She gave a wide-eyed look around the room silently suggesting Hettie would never allow such neglect.

Something flicked through Wade's eyes as if he had to shift horses in full stride to follow her comments. He looked around the room, stopped at the table and smiled. "Seems to me I recall white tablecloths and tall glasses courtesy of Hettie."

She looked at the odd assortment of dishes and the scrubbed wooden tabletop and shrugged. "A person is sometimes limited by the environment."

Wade chuckled as he turned his steady blue gaze to her. "I'd say the environment has improved considerably since last night."

Warmth crept up her cheeks at the way he looked at her as if her very presence made the house, the ranch and even the whole world a better place. She reminded herself how foolish such thoughts were, how stupid she was to build false hopes and expectations. But she failed to completely eradicate the sense of being appreciated and even admired.

"Thanks for cleaning the place." He cupped her shoulder making the feeling even more irrepressible.

The gesture was short-lived. She could almost believe she'd imagined it except for the way her nerves reacted, plucking at her heartstrings with such teasing insistence.

He stepped away to take his turn at the washbasin then headed for the table where Roy sat anxiously awaiting the food.

She'd set a place for herself after a brief struggle as

her pride did battle with her wariness and won. She would not allow her feelings to dictate her actions. She served the meal and sat across from Wade, Roy to one side. She glanced at Wade and he nodded. "I'll ask the blessing."

His prayer grew more confident each time. Suddenly, she wondered about his past. How could he be so confident and calm when he, of his own admission, had been made to feel like a nuisance, a dirty little boy as he put it? Had his mother managed to teach him to be strong in his faith despite their situation, or had he come to that strength later during the years he was on his own?

Did Scout fill a need in Wade's life that he failed to fill in Lucy's?

To keep her questions at bay, she passed the food, setting a serving aside to take to her father later.

Roy kept the conversation centered on the plans for the new barn, effectively leaving her to manage her confusion. Between comments, Roy devoured his food.

Wade ate a generous helping and took seconds and thirds. There would be no leftover corn bread for supper.

Roy eyed the pot she'd dished dessert from. "Can I lick the pot?"

"With your tongue?"

She felt especially pleased when Wade laughed.

"My tongue isn't long enough." No missing the regret in his tone.

"That's fine. I can wash it clean." She chuckled at his look of horror.

"It will be easier to wash if I clean it out good first."

"There's that. Sure, go ahead and clean it for me. I could use the help. But use the spoon on the cupboard. You'll get syrup all over your hair if you stick you head in the pot."

He jumped up and grabbed the pot, returning to his place. "I know you're teasing me but I don't care."

Wade laughed. "You're one smart lad."

Roy spared a moment to flash him a grin then gave his complete attention to cleaning the pot of every speck of syrup.

Lucy met Wade's gaze. They studied each other a moment. He gave a slow, steady smile so full of unexpected kindness that her mental reservations melted like butter in the sun. She could almost forget her vow to remain unemotional about this whole arrangement.

She jerked her attention to the empty bowl in the middle of the table. Her arms feeling wooden, she grabbed it and headed for the dishpan. She had work to do. That would keep her busy enough she wouldn't be able to waste her time dreaming about things that couldn't—wouldn't—be.

She took the plate of food to her father and returned immediately.

Roy and Wade pushed away from the table.

"Thank you for the great meal. Much appreciated. You did a good job." Wade sounded sincere like it was more than polite words.

She nodded. "You're welcome. Kind of you to say so."

He stood there, turning his hat round and round.

"Did I forget something?" She patted her hair as if searching for a mistake then glanced over her wardrobe. "Seems everything is in place."

She'd meant to be amusing but Wade didn't smile. "Lucy, you might try giving your father a chance."

Anger roared through her. She swallowed hard to control it, contain it. When she had it under control, she forced a grin to her mouth. "Cowboy, I suggest you throw your rope around someone else's affairs."

His expression hardened but not before she caught a glimpse of something. Be it disappointment or shock she couldn't say. She only knew it sent shame and remorse through her.

He slammed his hat on his head and headed for the door.

Chapter Eight

Wade grabbed the rifle from over the door as he hurried outside, away from Lucy. He'd ride out and find fresh meat. They could all use a good feed.

And he could use time to straighten out his thoughts.

He'd only been trying to help sort things between Lucy and Scout. She had no call to get snippy with him.

He saddled Two Bit and rode straight toward the bluffs. He reached his favorite spot and reined in to let his gaze sweep the vista before him. He could see for miles, clear to yesterday on one side, and all the way to tomorrow on the other. The sprawling view never failed to calm him and slowly his tension eased. He waited for the usual sensation that all was right with the world. No reason he should let Lucy get under his skin.

He sighed causing Two Bit to snort.

Lucy was already under his skin. The question was, what did he intend to do about it?

He sat staring into the distance. Seemed his options were pretty limited. They were stuck living in the same house as long as Smitty wandered free. After that...well, he wouldn't let himself consider what happened. 'Course it could be a long time before Smitty got corralled for one of his lawless deeds. Seems no one wanted to risk the man's anger by offering to testify against him.

In the meantime he was free to roam around intimidating people. It wasn't right. But he wasn't about to make Lucy and Roy the sacrificial witnesses. So that meant Lucy might be here awhile.

The idea sidled through him like sweet, refreshing water.

Lord, perhaps You could see fit to let her see me with a dose of kindness.

God had answered prayers before. Why, just a few days ago he'd asked for God to change Lucy's mind about coming to see Scout and look how quickly that prayer had been answered.

His mind clouded. A man had been shot. Lucy and Roy had been forced to run for their lives.

Maybe he should be careful about praying for things he wanted.

Something moved in the distance and he squinted to see it clearer. He could barely make out two tiny black objects, little puffs of dust convincing him they actually moved toward the south.

South. Toward the ranch. Could it be Smitty and one of his sidekicks? What was he thinking, leaving Lucy unprotected?

He reined around and bending low, galloped for home.

He barely waited for Two Bit to skid to a halt a few feet from the back door before rushing up the steps into the house. The kitchen was empty. "Lucy?" No answer.

He dashed into the living room. Scout lay snoring on the couch but a glance revealed no Lucy there either.

Where was she? Had they gotten here before him? It was impossible yet his heart beat double time as he raced back out the door and looked around. He saw his horse, the corrals, the low barn that was about to be replaced with a proper structure...but no Lucy. No Roy.

"Lucy," he bellowed. Did he hear voices toward the creek? He tipped his head. Was that Roy talking? He strode down the path through the little grove of trees. He broke through into the bright sunshine reflecting off the clear water where, pant legs rolled up, Roy waded in the creek.

He still didn't see Lucy. Wade's breath twisted in his throat before he finally spotted her hidden in the shadows, sitting with her back against a thin aspen. His chest heaved with relief.

What was she thinking? His insides steamed as he strode toward her. "What do you think you're doing?"

She tipped her head up and smiled though her eyes carried a hint of caution. She'd have to be dumb as the dirt at her feet to miss his anger. "Sitting in the shade?"

"Look around you. What's to stop someone from riding up unannounced? And you're..." He waved his hand. "Here."

"So I am. Enjoying the cooler air." She tipped her head back against the tree trunk clearly informing him she intended to continue her enjoyment.

Well, he knew how to end that. "I saw two riders headed this way."

The only sign she gave that it mattered was she opened her eyes. "Haven't seen them."

"Look, Lucy." Anger gave way to impatience. "How safe do you think it is to be sitting out here?"

"Look, Wade."

Her mocking imitation did nothing to ease his impatience.

"I guess I'm about as safe here as I am at the house. After all, there's you and my father to protect me."

Sure didn't sound like she thought they were

protecting her. Sounded more like they were annoying her.

"Sit down, you're giving me a crick in my neck."

Sit? Why he'd sooner...

He sat, hunched over his knees, a few inches from Lucy.

"How far can you see in any given direction?" she asked.

Even from the shelter of the trees he could see for miles. But he didn't answer her. He knew where she was going with this conversation and he didn't want any part of it.

She continued, her voice lazy. "I'm guessing about three days. Right?"

He gave a noncommittal sound. Let her decide if it was agreement or argument.

"So, I'm thinking if I don't walk around with my head in the dust at my feet, I should see any approaching riders in plenty of time to—" she shrugged "—well, do whatever. Right?" She nudged him in his ribs.

He shifted away and immediately regretted it. She was right. He'd overreacted. But he didn't like admitting it nor having her see it.

"There they are." He pointed to the pair of riders. "It's a couple of Indians."

She bolted to her feet. "Roy, get over here."

Wade laughed and caught her hand before she could tear away. "They won't hurt you. I recognize them. Usually they ride on by. Sometimes they come for a drink of water or coffee if there's any made. Hope you never have any corn bread lying about though. If they ever discover how good it is, they'll beat a path to your door."

She gave a strained laugh. "I'll never make corn bread again."

"I'm not suggesting that."

The riders looked toward the house but didn't turn away from their southerly journey.

"I expect they're headed for Lark." He tugged on Lucy's hand. "You're safe." She'd always be safe while he had anything to say about it.

A sigh rippled from her and she sank to the ground. "That scared me."

She still held his hand, erasing remnants of his anger and impatience. They sat in peaceful calm as Roy returned to playing in the water.

"Do you think there's any way Smitty can find us?" Her voice trembled and he knew she was truly worried when she let him pull her close to his side. Her head came to chin height. He had but to turn his face to feel wayward strands of hair touch his cheek and he closed his eyes at the sweet torture. He ached to rest his chin on the top of her head, press his hand to her hair and discover its silkiness. He swallowed hard and pulled his thoughts back to her concerns.

"I expect if he wants to bad enough he can find

us. He just has to ask the right people the right questions."

"You certainly know how to drive away my fears."

Her dry tone tickled him. "I can only promise to be on guard and protect you to the best of my ability."

She nodded, the movement brushing her hair against his cheek and—oh, mercy—driving all rational thought from his mind. If only they could sit here undisturbed by rational thoughts, unruffled by threats from Smitty, just peaceful and happy.

"I'm glad you don't make impossible promises." She shifted. "Did you bring any game?"

"Game?" His mind was as blank as the cloudless sky.

She jerked back to stare at him. "Didn't you go hunting? I was hoping for something to eat besides beans."

He scrambled to his feet, jeering at his complacent thoughts. "I hurried back when I saw the Indians. Didn't know—" He broke off. His eyes burned as he remembered his fear that something might harm Lucy. He tried to tell himself the fear didn't still linger in the dark corners of his heart. But knowing Smitty was out there somewhere, would likely persist until he found Lucy and Roy, would not allow the feeling to rest. It wouldn't until Smitty was locked up.

Lord, please give someone the courage to testify against him so Lucy will be safe.

Again he warned himself he should be careful what he prayed for. But no, God loved him. God loved Lucy and Roy. He could trust God to do what was best.

Tension slid out his body. "I'll go find some sage hens." He ducked through the trees. Two Bit stood patiently waiting. "Sorry, boy. Forgot about you." He led the horse to water and let him drink before he rode out to find some birds for supper.

Lucy stood in the shadows watching Wade. He'd come back, forgetting even his reason for riding out, just to make sure she was safe. To warn her to be watchful. The knowledge filled her with a sweet, fierce sensation. He was different than the other men she'd met and spent time with. But it didn't change the fact she only mattered to Wade because she was Scout's daughter.

She pushed aside regrets and longings. "Let's go back to the house, Roy." She waited for the boy to plow from the water and race toward her.

"This is sure a nice place. Guess we could do worse than stay here, don't you think?"

Stay. Here. With Wade. With her father. "It's not possible. Sooner or later we have to stop hiding and start living a real life."

Roy bounced around until he faced her. "You just don't want to stay because you're mad at Scout. How come, Lucy?"

She looked past Roy. What did she say to a boy who longed for family? Who craved attention so badly he lapped up the slightest kindness? She remembered feeling much the same way. Only she had Mama. And her faith. "Roy, people are never what we wish they could be. Best not to expect they will change. Like I told you before, God loves us and that's more than enough."

"No, it's not. I want someone I can hear and see. Someone with hands to touch me. Don't see God doing that, now, do ya? I expect that's why He made people. To do the stuff we can see and feel." He glowered at her a moment then raced off toward the barn to wave goodbye to Wade.

She wanted to call him back, warn him to guard his heart against wanting people to fill that need.

But he yelled something at Wade and waved until Wade was far out on the prairie.

She could only pray Roy wouldn't be hurt. And while she was at it, she prayed the same for herself. Her cheeks stung as she recalled how she'd let Wade hold her hand and promise to protect her. Her mouth twisted in disgust. As if she needed anyone to take care of her. Yet, she'd come perilously close to forgetting the fact.

* * *

Life settled into a routine of sorts. Scout was safely tucked away in the front room where she could, for the most part, ignore him. But all that had ended three days ago when her father insisted he was going to get up. It required Wade at his side to make it to the porch where he sat on a chair. "Sun feels good," he murmured, his eyes closed.

Roy hung about, his eyes wide and hungry, watching Scout. When he saw Lucy's warning look, he'd favored her with a scowl before he raced off to see what Wade was up to.

Lucy had returned to the kitchen feeling as if she was trapped. She didn't want to work on the porch with Scout out there. He made her feel too small.

Nor did she want to tackle cleaning the living room even though it desperately needed it. She didn't expect her father would want to sit up long and she didn't want to be caught on her hands and knees when he returned.

She'd mixed biscuits for supper. Wade had brought in more birds. The meat was welcome. She'd made stew with the old potatoes she found lingering in the cellar.

Two days ago, her father insisted he would join them for meals.

Lucy's nerves had tightened at the idea. But she could hardly refuse to eat with the men and Roy. So, she sat with Wade at her right side, her father at her left and tried not to wish—

She wouldn't let her thoughts go in that direction.

She had a life. She was content. This was only an interlude until Smitty could…what?

She could ride to Lark if Queenie would go that far and send a telegram to Dry Creek informing the sheriff of what she'd seen. Only when Smitty was locked up or hung would it be safe to return.

But she'd been around Dry Creek long enough to know Smitty had ways of finding out what he wanted to know. He would be watching the telegraph office. He would be after her before the sheriff read her message.

She'd have to run again.

On her own. She shuddered and glanced about to make sure she was alone.

Perhaps at some point she'd be ready to take that risk.

But not yet.

She wasn't ready to. And if she allowed herself even a fragment of honesty, she would be forced to admit it had nothing to do with the threat of Smitty finding her.

Not that she would admit she harbored forbidden dreams of having her father acknowledge her in a positive sort of way.

But even more honestly, she didn't want to walk away from Wade.

She sighed. Enough of this foolish rambling.

Today Scout had insisted he would go outside with Wade and Roy and inspect the preliminary work on the barn. While he was gone she intended to start cleaning the living room.

She scrubbed the floor within an inch of its life. Still, Scout didn't return so she made dinner. It was ready when the male members of this odd household returned.

"I'm hungry," Roy said as he rushed inside.

"Yup. Guessed you were." Wade laughed.

Scout scrubbed his hand over Roy's head. "A hearty appetite is a good thing."

Roy's food consumption must have triggered a sudden growth spurt because he seemed to grow six inches taller. His expression glowed with satisfaction as he beamed at Scout.

Lucy closed her eyes and prayed for patience to speak only kind words when anger threatened to fuel a burst of hurtful things. Roy was ripe for trusting, hungry for affirmation. He would do well to seek it from someone besides Scout.

The men ate quickly then pushed aside their plates and finished their coffee. Roy ate twice as much as anyone else but still managed to finish at the same time.

"Good meal," Wade said. "Thanks."

Scout pushed to his feet. "I think I'll watch you lay out the timbers."

"You sure you're up to it?" Wade asked.

"I can sit as well there as in here." Her father headed straight for the door but Wade paused at Lucy's side. "We'll be out all afternoon but back for supper."

It both surprised and pleased her that he thought to inform her. Just as he always spoke a word of thanks. She smiled. Her appreciation at his thoughtfulness sent a bolt of gladness to her lips. She didn't realize how eager she must look until Wade paused, his eyes wide, his gaze shifting from her mouth to her eyes and back.

Roy skidded after Scout. "Can I help?"

Wade dragged his gaze from Lucy. She felt an instant sense of relief. Or was it regret? He studied Roy. Roy had followed Wade everywhere since they first arrived so why he thought he should ask now...

Scout grinned at Roy. "We can always use an eager young fella."

Roy whooped, grabbed his hat and followed Scout outside.

"You'll be in the house alone," Wade said.

Again, his concern was such a marked contrast to Scout's unconcern that a smile settled in her insides even as it settled on her mouth. "I'll be fine."

He squeezed her shoulder before he followed Scout and Roy outside.

His touch remained, warm and steadying, after he left and she hummed as she gathered up the dishes.

A few minutes later Wade returned catching her still thinking of him. Her cheeks stung with embarrassed heat. "I thought you'd left."

"I have something for you." He grabbed her hand and led her to the back door and pointed to a triangle of metal he'd fastened to the corner of the eaves. "You need anything, you ring this." He handed her a length of metal. "Ring it until someone comes."

He'd thought of her long enough to make a way for her to signal him. She wanted to create a little room in her heart where the feeling she had this moment could last forever. She pushed reality to the forefront of her thoughts. "You think Smitty will track us down?"

"It's something we need to consider."

"I suppose it is. You keep an eye on Roy." She wished she could think of a way for him to signal her if he encountered trouble. But that was silly. He surely knew how to take care of himself.

He still stood on the open porch.

Slowly, first giving herself time to hide her concern or at least make it obvious it was only about Roy, she met his gaze. "Take care, hear?"

He brushed her cheek with the back of his finger. "You, too. Keep watch." He jumped off the porch and jogged to the low shed that served as the current barn.

She stared in the direction of the corrals, though her thoughts had gone on a trip that had nothing to do with horses or new barns. Something beckoned her heart. Something alluring and full of promise. She sniffed, realized she'd pressed her fingertips to the spot on her face Wade had touched and jerked her hand away. The only promises she believed were the ones in the Bible. What did the scriptures say? *Was God a man that He should speak and not do?* Even God knew the futility of trusting words given by a man.

Chapter Nine

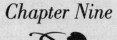

Their days settled into an uneasy pattern. Lucy cooked and cleaned, did the laundry and every now and then found time to wander down to the creek drawn by the murmur of the running water and the cool breeze.

Scout had taken to going out every day and supervising the barn construction. "He does more than I think he should," Wade commented several times.

Lucy didn't bother to say that from her experience, Scout did far less than she thought he should. But then they were talking about entirely different things. Wade meant work and health; she meant time and interest. Again, she reminded herself, the past was gone. Done. She had only the future to consider but it seemed life was on hold—waiting for whatever came next. She wished she knew what it might be. She knew her future was in God's hands, but still she often felt a restless stirring deep inside as if there was more and she was somehow missing it.

She sighed. It was only because being here reminded her too keenly of the pain of her childhood and made her forget the strength she'd found as an adult. *God, help me keep my eyes on You and what You promise.* The words of a familiar verse came to mind, "Jesus Christ, the same yesterday, and today, and forever." And she was comforted and strengthened to face the uncertain future.

It had been a few days since Wade brought in meat. He'd been busy working on the new barn. She missed the fresh addition to the meals. The limited supplies in the cellar hampered what she could make. But she wasn't about to complain about the hospitality offered.

Wade and Roy had come to the house for a drink of water.

Scout came from the corrals. Lucy had noted how thin he was—the aftermath of his illness. Over the past few days his color had lost its pastiness and his step had grown steadier. "Hey, Roy, I've been looking for you. Thought we'd go hunting together."

Roy jumped off the porch so fast Lucy feared he might break something. He raced to Scout's side, bouncing up and down on the balls of his feet. "Can I shoot the gun?"

Scout grinned. "We'll see. You want to help saddle my horse? We'll ride double."

The pair headed for the corrals, Scout tipping his head to catch every word Roy said. Scout's attention was good for Roy. Lucy didn't resent it a bit. She only wished she'd had even a fraction of her father's attention when she was a child.

She turned away and met Wade's quiet look. Quickly she shuttered her regrets and hurts. It was the past. It had nothing to do with who she was today. Or what she needed. She corrected herself. She needed nothing except a place to temporarily hide from Smitty. Last night she'd made up her mind to see how things lay in that direction and had written Hettie, hoping to post the letter in the near future.

"I planned to go to town." Wade sounded regretful.

That's what she needed most right now—to restock the pantry and post her letter. "I could sure use some supplies. The way the three of you eat, the pantry is emptying out real fast."

He sat down on the edge of the porch. "Can't go now."

"Why not?"

"Can't leave you here alone."

She didn't have to ask why. Smitty might track them here. Or the Indians might visit. She wanted to say she could look after herself but truth was, she didn't fancy encountering Smitty or any of his cohorts while alone or otherwise. As to the Indians, Wade's assurance that they were harmless failed to ease her nervousness at being alone should they come calling.

Wade sat in dejected contemplation.

"I wouldn't mind a trip to town." In fact, it sounded like the best idea since cold water. She and Wade on a trip together. *Stop. You know why you're here and so does he.*

"It's not a good idea for too many folks to know you're here."

She suddenly wanted to go to town so bad she could taste the dust of the trail. "I can be very discreet."

He sighed. "I need to get a few more things before we can go ahead with the barn. I don't want to wait until tomorrow."

She knew he was thinking out loud and let him come to the only reasonable conclusion.

"I guess if we don't advertise your presence too much you should be okay. You might enjoy meeting the woman who helps her husband run the store."

"Give me a minute to get ready." She rushed inside to get her letter. She told Harry and Hettie the whole story and knew they would keep her whereabouts a secret. They would also let her know if Smitty should move on or be arrested. If it was safe to return to Dry Creek.

She grabbed the only bonnet she'd brought and hurried out to wait for Wade who'd gone to get the horses. Only he pulled up in a wagon. Of course, he'd need something to carry supplies home in.

"I get to ride in style," she murmured as he helped her to the seat.

"I expect it will be better than Queenie."

She felt compelled to defend the faithful old horse. "I don't mind riding her."

"So long as you're not in a hurry."

She laughed and squirmed into a more comfortable position. No need to tell him she was in no hurry. This was the first time she'd been alone with him and she bubbled with anticipation. Perhaps they could talk about what they really wanted from life. Might be he wanted the same things as she.

Again, she drew a line across the path her thoughts headed down. She would not ever pin her hopes and dreams on what a man wanted or expected. Her father had taught her well the pain of doing so.

She sat up primly and faced forward turning her thoughts to the anticipation of a visit to town. "Tell me about the young woman at the mercantile."

He told her the couple had moved in and started the store six months ago, then he continued to describe the various businesses in town. She learned there was a supply store that brought in larger equipment from the east and lumber from the west. A school had been built the year before. She wished Roy had a proper home and could attend school. She'd fallen behind in teaching him to read and write and promised herself to tackle the job again.

They fell into pleasant conversation about barn building and the horses. They talked a bit about Roy. Wade wondered what happened to his parents.

"I don't think he remembers. Mr. Peterson got him from an orphanage to help with the work but he seems content to let Roy run wild so long as he does the chores. He doesn't feed him overly well or buy him clothes. Hettie found the pants he's been wearing and gave them to him."

"He needs a proper home."

On that she'd give no argument. But what a person needed and what they got were not always one and the same thing.

The conversation switched directions and nothing more was said about Roy's needs.

They drove into Lark. It was the first time she saw the town as they'd avoided it on their escape to the ranch. Now she had a good look. Two other wagons were tied at the side of the street as were several horses. Three men in conversation glanced up and nodded as they passed. She hoped they wouldn't take undue note of her presence.

The schoolhouse still looked raw and new. A scattering of houses stood behind the businesses. A new building gleamed white and fresh at the far end. "What's that?"

"Well, I'll be. Looks like the church got built. I wonder if they've started to hold services."

She promised herself she would find out and if she was still here come Sunday, she'd attend. Already she could hear the protests about keeping their presence a secret. But she didn't intend to be tied by a short lead rope. Not even for the likes of Smitty. What could he possibly do in front of a crowd of churchgoers? She shivered thinking of how alone she was at the ranch on many occasions.

But she would not let any man—not even an evil one like Smitty—make her afraid to live her life.

Wade pulled up in front of Lark Mercantile and helped her down. He escorted her inside and introduced her to Mrs. Styles. "Miss Hall is visiting her father."

He murmured low for her ears alone. "You stay here until I come back. Try not to talk to anyone else." His breath caressed her cheek and for a moment she forgot why he wanted her to be cautious, forgot they were not alone. She looked into his warning glance but for the life of her she couldn't get past how special it made her feel to have him want to protect her.

Then he was gone and she began to lecture herself for being so foolish. She didn't get a chance to finish as the woman he introduced came around the counter and took Lucy's hand. "Call me Marnie."

"And I'm not Miss Hall. I'm Lucy."

"How long are you here for? I hope you intend to stay. There are far too few women my age around."

She rushed on so fast Lucy didn't feel any need to answer her original question.

"Now what can I get you?"

Lucy produced her list and the letter to Hettie. Marnie talked nonstop as she filled the order. Within minutes, Lucy knew more about Marnie and her husband, Ernest, than she knew about just about anyone else in the world.

Marnie ground to a halt and started laughing. "You can tell I've been missing company of a woman my age. Now tell me about yourself. Where are you visiting from?" This time Marnie waited for Lucy to reply.

Lucy chose a vague answer. "From the east."

Marnie asked several more questions then she repeated her earlier one. "How long did you say you were staying?"

Lucy simply said, "It's a short visit. I see you have a new church."

"Oh, yes. How exciting. This coming Sunday is the first service. We still don't have a minister of our own but a preacher is coming for the service. I'm so excited. We haven't had regular church since we moved here in February. Why you'll still be here, won't you? You'll have to come."

"I'd love to if it's possible."

"Surely they'll both come."

Lucy blinked. She hadn't mentioned Roy. Then she realized Marnie meant Scout and Wade. She didn't say anything about Roy. Best if no one knew he was there. Someone asking after a woman and boy wouldn't care about a woman alone. So she only had to convince Wade that the two of them could go without sparking any interest.

"Tell me what you think of the countryside?"

Lucy smiled. "It's amazing. I feel like my heart expands just to encompass all the space."

"Some find it lonesome but I see you're a true prairie spirit."

Lucy sobered. She would soon be leaving these parts behind and returning to town life.

"How is Scout's barn coming along?"

"I heard them talking about bracing the walls and something about a ramp to lift the rafters."

Boots sounded on the wooden platform in front of the store.

"It's Wade." Marnie giggled. "If I wasn't married to a very nice man I might be jealous of you."

"Why on earth?"

Marnie rolled her eyes. "He's such a good man and so dreamy." She leaned closer. "And I see the way he's looking at you."

Lucy had turned to watch Wade approach but at Marnie's words found a sudden need to study the display under glass before her. "You're embarrassing me," she whispered.

Marnie only laughed. "I'll behave myself."

Wade stepped through the door. "Are you ready to go home?"

Home? The word grabbed at her heart and squeezed. She drew in a long breath and told herself home was back in Dry Creek, not on the ranch with Wade where the wind blew through the house and the scent of wildflowers filled her day. "I've gotten all I need for the pantry."

"I'll get a few things." He went to the men's ready-made wear and pointed out a few items to Marnie. She added them to the order.

On the way home, the wagon groaned under a load that included more lumber and a healthy amount of food supplies including two dozen precious eggs that Marnie had explained with a laugh were as scarce as hen's teeth. "You ought to get some hens of your own."

Lucy didn't bother to say she hoped to be gone before the two dozen eggs were used up. And she determinedly ignored the little tug she felt at the idea. Forcing her thoughts to other matters, she turned to Wade. "They're having their first church service on Sunday."

"That's good news."

"I'd like to go."

He gave her a startled look. "Do you think that's wise?"

"I thought about it. I figure if Roy and Scout stay

home no one will think twice about Scout Hall having a visitor."

He swallowed hard. "So, just the two of us go to church?"

Did he anticipate the idea as much as she? "Can't leave Roy home alone."

"No, 'course not."

She couldn't explain why it meant so much but it did. She loved going to church. She needed to attend to center herself again.

"I'll talk to Scout about it. If he agrees…"

She resisted an urge to hug his arm.

It was Saturday and if Wade wanted to escort Lucy to church he had to talk to Scout about it. Perhaps the man would object, stating the obvious—too many people knowing she was here put her at risk.

He watched Roy and Scout. Roy had sure taken to Scout and—for that matter—Scout to Roy. The older man seemed to delight in spending time with the boy, teaching him all sorts of things like how to ride a "real" horse. That brought a chuckle from Wade and he couldn't wait to tell Lucy her father's evaluation of Queenie. Her gaze had drilled into his with amusement and something he could only take as resistance.

"Lucy, why are you so suspicious of everything your father does?"

"I don't want to see Roy hurt or disappointed."

"Don't see how having Scout spend time with him should do that."

She shrugged and started to turn away then spun back, her eyes blazing. "You've known my father what? Ten months? Give me credit that I might know more about him than you do."

A hundred arguments sprang to Wade's mind but he bit them back. He allowed only one to find words. "Seems to me recent knowledge outweighs the past."

She stared lead bullets at him but he refused to flinch or turn away. "What happens when Scout decides he's had enough of Roy?"

"What sort of answer do you expect? That Roy will suffer for it? Or will he be better for the time he's spent with Scout? Lucy, there are no guarantees in life. You just have to take it as it comes."

She gave him a look of pure disbelief. "Is that what you do? Just take what life hands out and never complain? I suppose that's what you did when your mother's employers called you a dirty little boy? Just accept it. Well, I don't intend to sit around waiting for people—or life—to hand me what they choose. I'll make my own way, thank you very much."

He stalked away. She made him sound like a scaredy-cat shivering in the shadows meowing a squeaky protest over unkind treatment.

Out of sight of the house and Lucy's snooping gaze, he ground to a halt. He did his best to avoid trouble. What was wrong with that? Did she see that as running from problems? He didn't figure they were the same thing. Not even close. A fool rushed in with fists bunched at every imagined slight. A wise man avoided confrontation.

He leaned against the rail of the corral fence as a pain shafted through him. She'd made it clear she needed no one. That included him. He hung his head and waited for the agony to pass. Finally, it relented leaving his mind cleansed so he saw things clearly.

He wanted a chance to explain to Lucy how being unobtrusive had worked in the past but he would never stand quietly by if she needed him for anything. He would give his life for her if necessary. No, that might not be a good thing to say seeing as she emphatically needed no one. But perhaps going to church together would give them a chance to heal the rift caused by their spat.

So he must talk to Scout. Hopefully, the man wouldn't object too fiercely.

He found Scout with Roy, showing the boy how to measure and cut a perfect forty-five-degree angle.

"Hey, Scout, can I talk to you a minute?"

"Sure thing." He turned back to Roy. "Finish what I've shown you and I'll be back." He followed Wade into the shade of the old barn. "What's the problem?"

"No problem. Tomorrow is Sunday and the church

is finished in Lark. I thought I'd take Lucy to the service." He waited, expecting an argument.

"Roy?"

"I figure if no one knows he's here it will draw less attention to them. Thought you wouldn't mind staying home with him."

"Roy will be safe with me."

"That's settled then."

Scout nodded and hurried back to Roy who waited for him to check and approve his work. Wade stared after him, something vague and troubling scratching at the back of his mind. He couldn't bring it close enough to identify and with a shake of his head abandoned the nagging feeling.

Now all he had to do was announce to Lucy that he intended to take her to church.

He waited until after supper but before he could find the right words to say, Lucy collared Roy. "It's Saturday and you need a bath."

He looked liked she'd thrown a squirming snake at him. On second thought, he probably would have found that less disturbing. "Me and Scout have things to do."

"Fine. But before bedtime, a bath." She tipped her head and studied him. "And a haircut."

"I've got just the thing for you," Wade said, and retrieved a parcel from the loft.

Roy unwrapped the overalls and shirt Wade had purchased in Lark. His eyes grew wide. "For me?"

Wade nodded.

"They're brand-new." The kid sounded like the pockets were full of gold dust. "Thanks."

"You can wear them after your bath."

A rush of exasperation crossed Roy's teeth. "You sure do drive a hard bargain." And before Wade could do more than stare in surprise, Roy backed off the step, paused to give Lucy a fearful look then chased after Scout as if his life depended on it.

"That was very generous of you." Lucy's soft words of appreciation filled Wade with a mixture of sweetness and fear as he contemplated his next step. He needed a haircut as bad as Roy. Maybe Lucy would do him the honor.

The idea of Lucy cutting his hair filled him with a delicious sort of dreadful anticipation. He strode for the door and ducked outside before she could notice the sweat beading on his forehead. Getting her to cut his mop would provide a perfect opportunity to talk to her...though he couldn't think what they would talk about.

But he needed to clean up if he intended to go to the church service tomorrow. And he fully intended to. He looked forward with uncommon eagerness that to his shame had less to do with the fact they now had a church and a whole lot more to do with the idea of spending time with Lucy without Roy and Scout in attendance.

He snagged a bar of soap from the washstand Lucy

had set up on the step and headed for the pump house. Realizing he needed clean clothes, he went back to the house. Lucy seemed busy in her bedroom and he slipped inside and up the ladder to get a clean outfit without her notice. He'd prefer to sit in a tub but the idea of stripping naked in the house went beyond his sense of modesty. There was no way he could assure himself of privacy with Lucy nearby, so he filled a bucket and stood in the crowded well shack to soap up from head to toe. He shivered as he poured bucket after bucket of icy water over him until such time as he deemed himself clean.

He'd heard Roy and Scout head out presumably to hunt. The pair of them spent an inordinate amount of time traipsing around the countryside but he understood their enjoyment of freedom. Besides, it provided him opportunity to talk to Lucy.

He heard her humming as he returned to the house and toweled the water off the ends of his hair and finger combed it into place before hanging the wet towel over the bushes. He made a great clatter on the stoop to announce his return.

She stood at the counter slathering icing on a chocolate cake.

"You sure put those eggs to good use."

She jumped. "Marnie said the ladies were all bringing something on Sunday so everyone could enjoy a celebration feast afterward." She paused. "I didn't know if we were going but figured the cake wouldn't be wasted in any case."

She finished the task and set aside the icing bowl. "I'll save this for Roy to lick out." She faced him directly, skimmed her gaze over him, and smiled as a drop of water made its way down his earlobe.

He swiped it away. "I heard you mention something about a haircut."

"Roy is in need of one."

"Maybe you could cut mine, too? I'd like to look decent if we're to go to church." His throat dried so badly he almost choked before he finished the sentence. Then it threatened to close off entirely when he saw pink color flood up her neck clear to her hairline.

She didn't answer.

He wondered if she had the same throat problem he did. Perhaps it was something in the air. But he knew it was his heart causing the problem—he longed for her touch yet he feared how deep his feelings for her might go.

She sucked in air. "I've got no experience."

He assumed she meant at cutting hair. But he wished she meant at loving. He wanted to be her first love. Her last love. Her only love for as long as he lived. "I can hardly go to church looking like this."

She nodded, studying the hair at his collar with

a great deal of fascination as if she couldn't bear to meet his eyes. "I can give it a try."

"Good." He looked around, unable to think what to do next.

"Grab a chair and park yourself on the porch while I get the scissors."

He took a chair outside and straddled it backwards, hitching himself to the rungs like they were all that kept him from drowning.

She came out wielding a huge pair of scissors.

"I don't remember seeing those before."

"Don't suppose you would. I found them with some cleaning supplies." The way she said it and the grin she flashed informed him that anything associated with cleaning would not have garnered his attention.

He laughed. "Guess we neglected the house some."

"*Some* must have a different meaning in your vocabulary than in mine." She spread a tea towel around his shoulders, patting it into place.

He closed his eyes wondering if he could bear the sweet torture long enough to get a complete haircut.

"You praying?"

He chose to let her think so. "I think I'm going to need divine help."

She waved the huge shears. "You aren't in any danger physically..." The scissors flashed like a sword. "But I did warn you about my lack of experience. But then I guess everyone has to start somewhere." And she grabbed a chunk of hair and snipped.

His nerves jolted at her touch. He shuddered.

"Oh, come on. You'll live. If it's too bad, you can wear a hat."

"Not in church."

"I guess not." Another touch. Another snip. He gritted his teeth. This haircut business was not one of his better ideas. He grasped at something else to focus on. Anything else. The price of tea in China. The number of steps to walk from here to Lark and back. How many spikes it would require to put the barn together.

She edged around to cut the front.

He lowered his gaze but nothing but closing his eyes blocked her from his view. Closing his eyes did not stop his awareness but spared him the strain of watching her.

Her fingers brushed his forehead, filling him with such longing he didn't know if he could bear it much longer.

Her touch teased as she grasped bits of hair and snipped. He tried to concentrate on the pieces trickling across his face.

"There. It's about as good as I can get it." She scooped off the towel and flicked it over the edge of the stoop.

He tried to pull his senses into order with very little success. Tried to think of one sane thing to say. He glanced at her, fearful she would misinterpret his silence but she stared away from the house, so still he wondered if she saw something. Smitty?

"What is it?" He leapt to his feet, sending the chair dancing across the wooden platform. He rushed to the corner to study the landscape. He saw nothing amiss, not so much as a skitter of dust that might suggest a rider. "Did you see something?" Nothing out of place so far as he could see. Only Roy and Scout together in the trees.

She nodded, her gaze riveted to the pair. "Looks like they're building a tree house."

He wondered at the way her words choked out and studied her more closely.

Her eyes had a faraway look, the skin around her mouth white.

He wanted to touch her, bring her back from wherever she'd gone but something about her posture warned him how fragile she was and he hesitated for fear of frightening her.

"I remember—" She swallowed hard. "A tiny window I found discarded in a back alley." She fell back a step, her hand pressed to her throat. "Papa was visiting."

He blinked at hearing her call Scout Papa.

"Mama was so happy. Happier than she'd been in a long time, laughing and joking, making special dishes for Papa. I figured he must be very important to merit this kind of attention."

"Lucy?" He reached out and touched her.

She drew back another step.

Regret filled his lungs, making it impossible to breathe. He told himself she was lost in another world, another time but his rationalization did not open his airway.

"I was seven," she continued, her eyes wide and unfocused. "And shy in front of the man I adored. I showed him the window I'd found and he said, 'Lucy Loo, how about we build you a playhouse?'"

She jerked her head and fixed him with a look that seared across his brain.

"I didn't care if he built an upside-down outhouse if it meant he'd spend time with me." She looked past him allowing him to suck in hot unrefreshing air.

"I waited for him to find time. I gathered up scraps of wood. I planned how I would decorate my house. How he would join me for tea parties. Every morning I rushed to the kitchen to see if Papa was up. I hung back waiting for him to announce this was the day he would work on the playhouse. But he didn't even see me. And then one morning he threw his saddlebags over his shoulder and said, 'I'm on my way.'"

Her chest rose and fell rapidly as if she were chasing after her father.

"What about your playhouse?"

She shrugged. "It never happened." For just a

moment she met his gaze, let him see the unshed tears, the childhood pain and then her gaze hardened. "Now he's building a tree house for Roy."

She sighed. "Not that I care. It's too late for a playhouse. It's too late for tea parties. I no longer need or want one. I don't need—"

He watched the anger fade away to confusion. What had she been about to say? That she didn't need anyone? Hadn't she said as much already? And where did that leave him? "Thanks for the haircut. I think I'll look around."

He walked the perimeter of the yard to assure himself no one hung about.

Lucy called Roy and he and Scout tramped toward the house, Roy protesting all the way about the waste of water for taking a bath.

Scout ruffled Roy's hair and laughed. "Can't see it's going to hurt you any." Both he and Scout went inside.

Wade went to the tree house under construction. Had Lucy's ability to trust ended when her hopes and expectations had been dashed so many years ago? He couldn't believe it had. Wouldn't believe it. She only needed to see Scout had changed. And even if she didn't accept that, surely she could see she could trust him—Wade Miller. He never made promises he didn't intend to keep. Somehow, she must have seen evidence of that.

Wade remained among the trees, not wanting to

face the others. He longed to see a change in the relationship between Scout and Lucy. For his sake as much as theirs. Perhaps going to church would push her on her journey.

He let anticipation smooth his thoughts. A whole day for just the two of them. He intended to use his time well. *Lord, speak to her. Help her learn to trust so she can see love is waiting for her.*

Chapter Ten

Lucy carefully avoided looking at Scout as he and Roy came inside. "Your bath is ready," she told Roy.

"Aww. Do I have to?"

Scout laughed. "A good soaking never hurt anyone."

"You gonna have a bath?"

"Not in here. I'm heading for the creek." Scout snaggled a bit of soap and a towel and strode out of the house.

Lucy's shoulders dropped three inches and she sucked in air.

Roy launched himself after Scout. "I want to bathe in the creek, too."

Lucy caught him and turned him about. "Maybe when you're older. Tonight you're going to scrub right here and I'm going to cut your hair."

Roy grumbled the whole time she scrubbed him. Once he was dried, and wore the new clothing Wade had bought, she sat him on the chair outside and tackled his hair. At least she could relax as she snipped his hair. Not like cutting Wade's curls, which had proved sweet torture. The rough texture of it, the warmth of his skin, the teasing awareness of his closeness.

Just remembering set her heart tattooing against her ribs. For a few delicious moments she'd forgotten her vow to need and want no one. Then she'd seen Scout with Roy and it all came to a sudden halt. Now her insides were as knotted as neglected yarn.

She finished the haircut and let Roy run off to find Scout. As she cleaned up the bath things, she wished it were Sunday already. Perhaps in church she would find peace.

Later, the house quiet and she in her room, she pulled out her mother's Bible. She wouldn't be able to sleep until she'd put to rest the myriad emotions tangling her mind. *Lord, speak to me. You have promised peace that passeth understanding. I could sure use some of that right now.*

She turned the thin India paper pages and tried to think where she could find what she needed. But not even knowing what it was she sought, she couldn't begin to guess where to look.

Closing the Bible and shutting her eyes, she paused, aching for the Lord to speak comfort to her soul. Then she let the pages fall open and lowered her gaze. She read Psalm one hundred and eighteen. At verse twenty-four, she stalled. *This is the day which the Lord hath made; we will rejoice and be glad in it.*

"Thank you, God," she murmured. This was what she needed to keep in mind. The past was over. Gone. Done with. It could hurt her only if she dwelt in it. Today was full of good things.

She was an independent young woman.

She and Roy were safe.

They were in a pleasant setting. She let her thoughts drift to her favorite spot by the creek, let them go further to the endless spaces of the prairie.

She had a friend in Wade and best of all—she gave a secret smile—she and Wade were going to church tomorrow.

She rose the next morning, eager for the outing. Not even the fact Scout didn't bother to glance at her, or note how she'd done her hair up with pins she'd purchased at the store dampened her enthusiasm. Long ago she'd accepted he didn't notice or acknowledge her. The fact had lost its power to sting especially when she saw the eager light in Wade's eyes.

Yes, this was going to be a good day.

We will rejoice and be glad in it.

A cool breeze and a cloudless sky promised a beautiful Sunday morning as Wade helped Lucy onto the wagon. He took his place at her side and smiled at her. She looked fine indeed. She wore a dress he'd seen before—a pretty red print with full sleeves and a lace-trimmed collar. He realized she had only three dresses with her yet she always looked as fresh as a newly blossomed flower. She wore her customary braid only she'd pinned it into a circle around her face that made her look elegant as a princess.

As she returned his smile the sun touched her cheeks with faint pink. "I'm ready."

He grabbed the reins. He'd been staring at her long enough to cause her both amusement and embarrassment. They rode several minutes before he could pull his thoughts into some semblance of intelligence. It wasn't that he didn't have things he wanted to say but his thoughts rushed the gate in general disarray.

"Nice day." It wasn't one of the things crowding to be said. It was a stupid, pointless comment. What other reply could she give besides yes or no? It got him not one inch closer to expressing the things crowding his heart. "I expect there will be a good turnout for church." And how did that help? He restrained a desire to punch the side of his head. *Think before you speak, man.* "Hope we don't have to stand outside." He stifled a groan. When had he become so thickheaded? He scraped his teeth over his tongue. It felt like his but it acted like he'd borrowed it from a dull stranger.

"I don't care so long as we can join in the singing and hear the sermon. I really feel in need of both."

He chortled. "Don't think you want to include me in the singing. I'll be content to listen."

She flashed him a sunny smile. "I can't believe you sing as bad as you say."

"Believe it."

"Someday I'll get a chance to judge for myself."

Their gazes locked at the promise of someday. His heart filled with expectation. Then she seemed to realize what she had said. Her expression tightened and she faced forward.

"Someday might never come." He tried to keep his tone light as if still joking about his singing but his thoughts had shifted to so much more than that and he guessed from her reaction hers had as well.

Again, he tried to corral his thoughts, chase them to the gate in an orderly fashion. There were so many things he wanted to say, ask, discover but he couldn't sort his thoughts into a row. Finally, one question surfaced. "What do you think of the prairie?"

"Lived on prairie most of my life but always in town. Never gave it much study until I came here. There's something about living where you can see for miles in every direction."

"You like it?"

"Yeah. I do. It makes me feel…I don't know. It's hard to explain. I guess I feel bigger, freer." She sighed expansively. "When I go back to Dry Creek

I will miss looking out the window and seeing the openness. I can't even see out my window at Harry and Hettie's. It's way up toward the ceiling."

One anxious thought settled back in relief. He'd heard of women who hated the wide-open spaces. But Lucy gal would miss them. He hoped she'd miss a few other things, as well. Like maybe a certain cowboy.

"You don't have to go back." There. He'd brought it out in the open. His lungs refused to work as he waited for her reaction.

She laughed. "I have a job back there I like very much."

He sucked air over his teeth. That wasn't the answer he hoped for. He decided to push the idea a bit further. "Scout could use a full-time housekeeper. I guess you saw that soon enough." He barely stopped a groan. He didn't want her to stay to be a housekeeper for Scout. That wasn't his wish at all.

She studied him a full moment, her eyes steady and searching.

He let her look, let her gaze go deep into his soul hoping, praying she'd see what he wanted to give her even though he had neglected to say it clearly.

She blinked and shook her head. "I can't stay."

"Because of Scout?"

She stared straight ahead. "Because of me. Because I will never let myself—"

He waited for her to finish but she sighed and said

no more. After a few minutes he settled into glum silence.

Soon other wagons of various sorts as well as men on horseback filled the road. He hung back several yards from the nearest wagon to avoid breathing the dust getting kicked up.

He joined the parade down the main street of Lark to the church. "Where did all these people come from?" He had no idea there were so many in the area.

He found a place to leave the wagon and helped Lucy down. She carried the cake as she glanced around, her eyes bright as she took in the people hurrying toward the church. They made their way to the door, pausing often to meet and greet neighbors and friendly strangers. Someone took the cake from her and carried it away.

Inside the church, they squeezed into a pew. The few empty places filled up quickly. As Wade expected, latecomers would be left standing outside.

A very young man stood and introduced himself as the preacher from over at Big Springs. They had no organ or piano so they sang without the aid of instruments. Wade enjoyed the blend of voices—especially Lucy's clear sweet tones.

She shot him a teasing look as he sat silent, listening. The way she wiggled her eyebrows as if daring him to join in almost made him laugh. She'd regret it if he let out so much as one sour note.

The young preacher boy stood to deliver the sermon. Wade didn't expect the preacher had enough experience to have anything of value to say but within five minutes he realized his mistake. The man spoke of hardship and disappointments. He'd obviously had his share of both.

"They can make us bitter or make us better. We have the power to decide which. Don't let your problems drive a wedge between you and your loved ones. Between you and God. Choose forgiveness. Choose love."

Wade vowed he'd never let things make him bitter. *What if Lucy returns to Dry Creek and you never see her again?*

A deep bone-crunching loneliness hit him at the mere idea. *Lord God, may these words speak to her heart. Help her find a way to choose forgiveness.*

The service ended and the congregation moved outdoors where plank tables had been set up.

The men gathered in little knots as the women hurried to put out the food.

The young preacher called for their attention and offered up a prayer of gratitude for God's many blessings. Wade murmured, "Amen." God's blessings were beyond measure. And if God so chose, the blessings would continue.

His gaze sought and found Lucy, surrounded by a gaggle of women. He could enjoy seeing her every day of his life.

What would it take to convince her to stay?

Or perhaps he could find contentment at a job in some town for he knew despite her claims to a home and job in Dry Creek, she could not return while Smitty walked free.

But he knew it wasn't Smitty or the place he chose to live that created the barrier between them.

It was the feelings she'd stored up from her past—hurts and misunderstandings Scout had inflicted.

If only she and Scout could forgive the past.

Lord, show them the way.

As families with young children were urged to the front of the line, Lucy came and stood at his side. He ached for the right to touch her, pull her near, lean close and smell the honey scent of her hair.

But he didn't have the right and would not act inappropriately, shaming them both.

They filled their plates from the bounty. He made sure he got a piece of Lucy's chocolate cake then they found a place near one of the trees, clinging to the meager shade. Conversation lulled as people concentrated on the food.

Wade devoured Lucy's chocolate cake. "Mmm. Good."

"I doubt it's as good as Mrs. Adam's."

He remembered the cake she'd raved about at the literary evening back in Dry Creek. "I wouldn't know, having never had so much as a taste." He gave her a pained look reminding her how she'd hoarded the whole thing.

She giggled. "You'll have to take my word for it."

He sobered suddenly, reminded sharply of the issue of trust. "Lucy, if you say Mrs. Adam's cake beats this, I believe you. Maybe if I say this is the best I've ever tasted you'll believe me. Can you take my word for it?" If she did it was a step toward trusting him on other things—like love.

She tipped her head and her eyes sparkled with mischief. "I guess I'd be willing to believe you haven't eaten a whole lot of chocolate cake."

He understood her qualified agreement. She could believe only a little bit. It was a start. He wished he felt better knowing it.

A gust of wind tore across the yard, picking up hats and bonnets and baby blankets. A black bonnet skittered by. Wade leapt after it at the same time as Lucy. They banged heads as they reached for it.

Wade grabbed his forehead. "Ouch."

Lucy grunted. "You have a hard head." She stumbled backward.

Wade grabbed her shoulder and steadied her. "Are you hurt?"

"I don't think so." She clung to his arm as the wind whipped about them tugging her braid free, sending pins scattering.

"Oh, no. I've already lost most of my pins."

He searched for them, found four and handed them to her. Their fingers brushed. He forgot the others. "Lucy—"

"My bonnet." An elderly lady hustled toward them. "You stopped it. Thank you." She fluttered her hands toward Wade. "Why you must be the young man who is working with Mr. Hall."

"Wade Miller, ma'am."

"I'm Mrs. Thomas. Widow Thomas. And this young lady is your wife?"

Lucy backed up in alarm. "Oh, no, ma'am. I'm Scout Hall's daughter. Just visiting for a few days."

Wade's feelings dropped into a bottomless cave. Did Lucy have to act like the idea of being his wife was a fate worse than hanging?

Widow Thomas narrowed her eyes and squinted at Lucy. "You're going to be married soon?"

"No, ma'am. I'm just visiting." She emphasized each word with a shake of her head. "I'll soon be gone."

Mrs. Thomas fixed a beady look on Wade. "I expect you'll persuade her otherwise."

"Yes, ma'am," he said. It was his heart's intention.

"No, ma'am," Lucy said.

The widow Thomas smiled at Lucy and patted her hand. "Welcome to the community. I'm sure you'll like it here." She donned her hat and marched off.

Lucy chuckled. "I don't think she got it sorted out at all."

"Guess not."

"What's wrong?"

"Did you have to make it sound like I have a dreadful disease or something?"

"I didn't."

Others were leaving. "Get your things."

She hesitated then went to the table.

He waited, took the empty cake plate and the eating utensils she'd brought and led the way to the wagon. He'd had other plans for the afternoon but now he couldn't wait to get home.

She settled on the seat and waved goodbye to the others. They headed out of town. "Wade, I was only trying to make her understand the truth."

"You did a good job." She might as well have signed and sealed his doom. Obviously, the idea of being his wife sat like a splash of sour milk in her thoughts.

She touched the back of his hand. "I didn't mean to hurt your feelings."

"Of course you didn't." She just didn't see past her own mistrust of commitment. "Do you plan to be single all your life?"

His question seemed to startle her. She started to speak and then paused as if she needed to consider the answer.

"I—I don't know."

At the catch in her voice, he reconsidered his plans. Perhaps she was in a mood to discuss things. He badly wanted to deal with the way things were between them though he wondered if the sweet tension he felt was one-sided.

He turned off at a side trail. She seemed not to notice. His anger melted at the misery in her posture. "Lucy gal, a person can get mighty lonely by themselves."

She huffed. "Guess you forget how many people come into the dining room each day. I don't foresee being alone a problem."

"How many of them keep you company in the evenings? How many care how you're feeling? Who takes time to listen to your concerns? Lucy gal, who holds you when you need it?"

The way she sucked her lips in, he knew he'd touched a raw nerve. He wasn't sure he liked it and reached for her hand. At first, she stiffened and acted like she would jerk away and then she settled into letting him hold it. It felt as good and right as rain on a Saturday afternoon after the week's work was done.

"I'm not meaning to upset you. I only want you to see where your choices are taking you."

They neared the river and she sat up and looked about. "Never mind where *I'm* taking me. Where are *you* taking me?"

"To the river. Is that all right?"

"Don't suppose there's any need to rush back. The place got along without me before I came and will get along just fine after I leave."

It wasn't exactly the message he wanted to hear but he let it go as he pulled up by the trees and jumped down. She readily let him lift her down, apparently all discord forgotten in her eagerness to explore.

He took her hand and led her through the cottonwoods to the edge of the river.

She breathed deeply. "I love the sound of running water. Can we walk?"

There was no path but the grassy embankment allowed easy navigation. She continued to let him hold her hand and he simply enjoyed the moment. They came to a fallen tree. He planned to assist her over but she sat down.

"This is a really nice place."

"I agree." He was glad he'd chosen to come here. There was that word again—choice. Seems it had been a theme throughout the morning. "Did you enjoy the church service?"

"Immensely. You?"

"Very much. I wondered what such a young fellow would have to say but he delivered a good message."

"I agree."

He laughed at her imitation of his earlier response. "It's sobering to realize how profoundly our choices can affect our lives."

"What sort of choices did you think about?"

"One that came to mind for me was the one I made to live as my mother taught me even when I was among those who mocked my choices. I didn't go into town and spend my wages on drinking and carousing. I didn't buy silly things. I suppose in some ways that choice kept me out of trouble. I didn't mind the ribbing of the other cowboys not even when they called me a Goody Two-shoes."

She squeezed his fingers. "They teased you? About what?"

He shrugged. "I wouldn't swear. And I preferred to go to church instead of to the saloon."

"I guess the teasing must have hurt."

"At first. Then I suppose I got used to it. I did think a couple of times about pretending I wasn't a Christian but I always thought of how disappointed my ma would be and thought better of it. But still my faith seemed secondhand until this winter when I prayed and God rescued me. Now I'm learning to choose to trust God in my life." He turned her hand over and examined it, running his finger along each finger to her wrist. "You know when that preacher talked about choices, I thought of you."

She would have jerked her hand away except he suspected she'd try and tightened his grip.

"Are you going to try and change my mind about going back to Dry Creek?" Her voice carried a challenge.

"Could I?"

Her gaze darted away from his then returned and remained, seeking answers.

He didn't know if he had them.

He read her confusion, her hesitation and her hurt then she shook her head and turned her gaze toward the water. He dragged air over his teeth and continued. "Because if I could persuade you, I would." How desperately he wanted to keep her with him forever.

Her lips parted but she didn't speak.

"Lucy gal, you know I want you to stay. Because I care about you." He'd said it plain. She'd have no mistake in understanding his feelings.

She held so still, so quiet he wondered if she searched for a way to avoid his words. Then she lifted her head and her eyes shone with what could be surprise or happiness. Either worked for him.

His gaze slipped to her lips. He lowered his head, didn't hide his intention to kiss her; gave her lots of time to stop him. She didn't. In fact, he knew he wasn't imagining how she leaned forward to meet him.

The kiss was short. It filled his heart with unfamiliar sweetness that rolled up his throat and flooded his brain. He couldn't stop smiling as he pulled back.

Her eyes were wide, full of surprise and delight to equal his own.

Then she gave a strangled cry and jumped to her feet.

Chapter Eleven

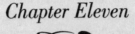

Lucy tried to run. The grass caught at her feet. She would have fallen except Wade caught her and spun her around to face him.

"What's wrong?"

She rolled her head back and forth. "I can't stay." She couldn't fall in love. She couldn't give the care and keeping of her heart to another. She knew too well the cost. Wade wasn't Scout but it made no difference. Loving, trusting, hoping, led to hurting and heartache.

"I'll take you home."

She didn't care if he thought she meant she had to leave the river or if he knew she meant the ranch. All that mattered was getting away from this intimate place. Only it wasn't Wade she needed to escape. It was her foolish heart. How could she have let herself slide into such a precarious state that she'd actually considered what it would be like to stay with Wade? She had even gone so far as to welcome his words. *I care for you.*

It was Widow Thomas's fault for going on about being his wife.

Only it wasn't. Her own foolish heart found something in Wade that she'd wanted all her life.

She wouldn't allow herself to think what it was.

Wade held her elbow as they retraced their steps. She would have to be in a semiconscious stupor to not notice she'd displeased him. She didn't care for his anger any more than his confession of love. She corrected herself. He hadn't said he loved her. Only that he cared. Well, no doubt he cared about his horse, too. She didn't need to read too much into it. Nevertheless, she wanted to put things back on a less emotional basis.

"Roy will fear he might starve if I'm not back to make supper."

Wade stopped moving and his grasp on her elbow stopped her, as well. "This has nothing to do with Roy."

"What are you talking about?"

"You're afraid to trust. You blame Scout because he disappointed you but the truth is it's like the preacher said—you've made choices and you cling to them."

She pursed her lips as anger surged through her. She sucked in air until she felt in control. "Well,

Mr. Know-It-All, exactly what sort of choices do you think I've made?"

He leaned closer so they were almost nose to nose.

She would not retreat.

"Lucy gal, you decided to never trust another person—or maybe just another man. You decided you wouldn't allow anyone to get close for fear they might hurt you."

His words were so accurate she gasped and then pressed her lips together lest he guess he'd struck the bull's-eye.

He nodded. "And you haven't stopped to think it's keeping you from all sorts of wonderful things."

"Huh. Like what?"

"Like a chance to enjoy having a pa. Like a chance to be loved." He grunted and stalked away.

She stared after him. "Who says I want to be loved?"

He glared over his shoulder. "Everyone does."

She wanted to dispute his assurance but she couldn't speak as longing welled up inside her so insistent, so overwhelming she couldn't move.

He strode onward.

She pulled herself together and hurried after him. "Sometimes," she muttered, "a person has to learn to live without love."

She hadn't meant for him to hear and drew to a stop when he turned.

"No, a person chooses to live without love. And it's a mighty lonely life, if you ask me."

So, who asked you? She kept the thought inside her head.

His anger faded. He reached for her.

She knew she should back away, not allow his touch. It would upset her resolve. But she couldn't deny herself the contact. She'd learned to lock her emotions into a secure room but there were times she wanted things she'd denied herself, times when she simply ached to belong to someone.

"Lucy gal." His soft words almost broke down the locks on her secret room. "I must respect your choice. I can only pray something will change your mind."

Let him pray all he wanted. She couldn't see how it would change anything. Sometimes a person just had to live with what they were. But never before had she even considered she might need to change, let alone be able to.

Wade smiled and took her hand. "Come on. Let's go home."

Wade lingered at the table. Since their Sunday outing last week, he'd looked for every opportunity to be near her. He sensed a delicate change between them as if his words had challenged her carefully constructed fences.

She stood in the open door. He slipped over to stand behind her, needing to be as close to her as possible even though she'd done nothing, said nothing to encourage him.

He followed the direction of her gaze to where Roy and Scout worked on the tree house.

His glance at Lucy revealed exactly what he expected to see—hurt and confusion. He wished he could erase it with a touch or a kiss. "The barn is coming along great. The walls are about ready to go up."

She nodded.

"Scout knows his way around a hammer and a piece of wood."

Another nod. But he felt her careful attention as she tried to guess where he was going with this conversation.

"I'm learning lots from him. He's teaching Roy as they work on the tree house. The boy will at least know how to cut a piece of wood and nail it straight when they're done."

She didn't say anything but he felt her tension as if she wanted to and waited, giving her lots of time to speak her mind. And he prayed for God to open her heart to the good things about Scout.

Finally, she sighed. "I hope all he gets is some practical skills." Turning, she came face-to-face with Wade and her eyes widened.

If he wasn't mistaken it wasn't only surprise that filled her eyes. He was certain it was more when her gaze darted to his lips and her breath caught audibly. She swayed toward him.

He caught her shoulders and steadied her although he wanted nothing more than to pull her against his chest and promise her his love, his fidelity, his protection—everything he had and was. Caution stopped him. He understood she was dealing with choices made in childhood, realized they were hard to change. He didn't want to rush her as he had last Sunday by the river.

Perhaps if they could have gone to church again….

But without a preacher of their own, services were only scheduled for once a month.

Determination hardened her eyes and tightened her mouth. She stepped away. "I need to set the yeast for lightbread." She mashed the potatoes as if they deserved all her frustration and confusion, added warm water, two cakes of dry yeast and flour enough to make a runny mixture.

He'd seen his ma do this many times and knew Lucy would stir the bubbles down before bed and in the morning add enough flour to make bread dough.

Contentment seeped through his troubled thoughts as he watched her. Life should be like this—a quiet sharing of daily tasks, enjoying each other's company.

Roy raced into the house and guzzled a dipper full of water. "I'm going to put on the roof tomorrow."

Scout followed at a more sedate pace. "I'll have to go to town and buy some more five-penny nails for Roy."

Lucy's head jerked up. Her gaze bored into Wade, alive with relief.

Did she find Scout's presence so difficult to bear or—he licked suddenly dry lips—was she anticipating having Wade to herself? Roy couldn't go to town but one could count on him spending hours at his tree house.

Scout left early the next morning. Lucy watched him go without any regret. So long as he hung about, larger than life, his voice carrying to her from different areas of the yard, she could not put him from her troubled mind. Since she had attended church with Wade she'd fought hard for peace of mind. Her inability to trust her father—who had proved over and over he didn't want or deserve her trust—did battle with the things Wade had said about making choices that shut others out. And it warred mightily with the feelings harbored in secret places at Wade's kiss.

Since Sunday, Wade had seemed to forget they'd argued—for which she was grateful. He also seemed to have forgotten he'd kissed her. She didn't find that quite so acceptable.

Perhaps if they could spend some time together she might sort out her confusion.

She'd expected Roy to be occupied with his tree house. Instead, he produced a bat and ball.

"Where did you get that?" she asked.

"They're Scout's. He said we could play with them."

"We? Play?" Wasn't exactly what she had in mind.

"Sure. The three of us." He looked from Wade to Lucy, his expression eager.

Lucy glanced at Wade. Did she see the same hesitation she felt? Had he, too, hoped for a chance to be alone, to talk, perhaps kiss?

Roy rushed on. "We can play scrub, can't we? I seen some boys playing it in an empty lot back at Dry Creek. I wanted to join in but they didn't let me."

Lucy knew she couldn't say no after that.

Wade sent her a regretful look and shrugged. "We'll play with you." He caught Lucy's elbow as they headed to a level area a few yards from the house. "Do you know how to play?"

She laughed. "I know how to play jacks, jump rope, hide-'n-seek...." She trailed off after mentioning girlie games. "But I have also played ball a time or two in school."

"Good."

"Just remember how long ago it was."

"Oh, indeed. Years and years."

She giggled. "Seems like years ago. So much has happened." She draped her forearm across her forehead in a dramatic gesture.

"Now that's more like the Lucy gal I first saw." He caught her hand and swung their joined arms.

She scowled. "Are you saying I've grown sour and grumpy?"

He pressed his palm to his chest. "My dear, why ever would you accuse me of such a horrible thing? You've been the perfect model of sweetness."

"Huh." She didn't need him to point out that if not sour and grumpy, she'd been quieter than normal. But today would be different. She could relax with Scout gone.

Roy raced ahead and placed a piece of wood for the batter's plate and another for first. He tossed the ball overhead and swung the bat in an arc that went downward.

"I think the boy could use some coaching," Wade murmured. "Why don't you pitch and I'll show him how to bat?"

"I'll try but be warned that I throw like a girl."

His grin threatened to split his cheeks. "Can't hardly imagine why."

Laughing, she scooped up the ball and faced Roy. Wade stood behind Roy, wrapped his arms around Roy and grasped the bat, showing Roy how to hold it.

Lucy's first pitch was perfect—if Roy was ten feet tall. The next one better suited a grasshopper.

Wade straightened and tipped his hat back to scratch his head. "Here's the batter." He patted Roy's hat.

"I know." She scowled.

"Was wondering, is all. Seems you might of mistook something else seeing as your pitches were...a little wild."

"Watch this one." She narrowed her eyes and focused on the target area, determined not to let Roy's wide-eyed fright nor Wade's chuckle distract her. She threw the ball and it came within reach of Roy's bat. Wade helped him swing and the bat connected with the ball.

"Run," Wade yelled. "Go for first."

Lucy scrambled for the ball, waited until she was certain Roy would make it safely to the base then tossed it to Wade.

"You're safe. Now wait until I hit a fly ball and you can run home."

Lucy gave a long-suffering sigh. "I can see I'm going to be here a long time trying to get the pair of you out."

Roy giggled. Lucy winked at Wade letting him know she didn't mind one bit so long as Roy had fun.

Wade rolled his eyes. "You have to play to win."

"Oh, yeah." She threw the ball as hard as she could. A bit wild. In fact, it would have hit him if he hadn't jumped back and swung the bat at the same time. The ball went straight up and she ran to catch it. Play to win? She'd show him she could.

Wade ran toward first, hollering at Roy to run for home.

Her gaze on the soaring ball, she ran toward the batter's plate, crashing into Wade. He grabbed her, staggering as he kept them both from falling to the ground.

Her breath raced in and out more from the way Wade's arms felt around her than from her run. She forced herself to take slow easy breaths as her fear tangled with her reaction.

She could not, would not risk her heart. Even if she felt tempted otherwise. The pain was not worth the pleasure.

She pulled herself away from his grasp and returned to the game. They played until they were hot and sweaty then headed for the pump to cool off and get a drink.

Roy swiped his arm across his mouth. "That was fun. If we stayed here I think we could always find a way to have fun."

Lucy grabbed his shoulder. "We aren't staying. Once it's safe, we'll go back to Dry Creek or some place else." The words came by rote. Somehow she couldn't make them mean as much as they once had.

"I ain't going back. You can't make me."

"No, I guess I can't." Any more than she could

prevent him from building impossible dreams based on what he might get from Scout. "But I'm not staying."

Roy turned to Wade. "I'm going to make her change her mind."

Wade chuckled. "How you going to do that?"

"She likes it here. I know she does. I seen the way she smiles when she looks out the window or stands at the door." Roy tipped his head as if studying the matter. "Guess I could do something to make her see what she'd be missing if she left." His face brightened. "Like bring her flowers. She loves the wildflowers."

Wade stared at the boy with respect. "Why, Roy I believe you've hit on an idea. You'll make someone a fine husband some day."

Roy backed away, a look of horror on his face. "I ain't never getting married."

Wade laughed. His gaze sought Lucy's, full of warmth and promise and—

She jerked away. "Can't live on dreams, Roy."

"Guess I can if I want. You the one what told me we all need to be loved. Well, I guess this is as close as I ever been." He stomped off toward the tree house.

Lucy wanted to call after him, warn him how he could be hurt. She turned to Wade thinking to explain her reasons but Wade picked up the bat and ball and headed for the house. He stored the equipment behind the door then leaned against the door frame and studied her.

She didn't move. Couldn't move as her thoughts zigzagged across her brain.

We all need love. Hadn't Wade said something like that? And hadn't she stubbornly insisted she didn't? Only it wasn't so much she didn't need or want love. It was she had so long denied her feelings she didn't know if she could change what she'd become.

Did that mean she had opened her heart to the possibility?

Lucy scrubbed at her eyes. If only she could go back and adjust her choices.

She wanted Wade to understand. "I don't want him hurt. Children don't have the wisdom of adults so they make choices that seem right in their inexperience. Later, they begin to see the foolishness of their choice. But sometimes it's too late to change."

She felt his careful consideration of her statement and appreciated he didn't immediately dismiss it.

"I understand how that could happen. A child thinks as a child. But an adult needs to put away childish things and reason as an adult."

His words both gave her hope and sent long fingers of fear into her bones making them ache. "Isn't that from the Bible?"

He gave a lopsided grin at her. "Loosely."

"Isn't that like asking a zebra to leave his stripes behind and become a donkey?"

"Not if he's a donkey in the first place and only thinks he's a zebra."

"We aren't really talking about donkeys, are we?"

"No, Lucy gal. We're talking about people." His eyes crinkled at the corners in gentle affection. "I think we're talking about you."

She wanted to deny it. "I don't know if I'm a donkey or a zebra."

His smile edged between her worries and her hope, blocking the former and allowing the latter to thrive. "You are a beautiful woman with a heart capable of loving and trusting. But you've locked that big heart of yours behind walls of fear and mistrust."

Beautiful? Big heart? Did he really believe that? "It's the only way I know."

"But you no longer need those walls."

At the way he smiled, silently promising so much, she sensed a crack threatening her secure walls. Was it possible for them to crumble? She recalled his words on their journey to the ranch, promising he would always be there for her. Were his words enough to enable her to demolish the walls? What happened if she let the barriers down only to find he didn't give anything more than her father had? From the depths of her soul she knew Wade did not deserve to be slipped into the same slot as her father.

"Lucy gal, you are an adult now. You can reason things through and change how you look at them."

"Is it possible to change?" Her whisper came from a secret place that still hoped and still ached for love.

Wade took her hands. "I wish I could tell you what you need to do in order to change but I don't know what you need. I pray you will find the way." He brushed his fingers over her cheek, pulling an errant strand of hair off her face.

She leaned into his touch as inside grew a shimmering sensation of possibility.

He kissed her forehead.

She closed her eyes. With his encouragement, she could face anything. Even her fears. But it wasn't enough. If she let down her barriers, she had to be able to face the consequences with or without his strength. Was she strong enough?

She kept her head tipped. She couldn't meet his gaze, couldn't let him see how vulnerable she was at the moment. It would take very little urging on his part to push her past the confines of her secure boundaries.

Chapter Twelve

Wade wanted to kiss away all her fears, get her to confess she didn't need a blitz of attention from Scout in order to realize she wanted to stay. He wanted to be the reason. He wanted to be enough. His thoughts jolted against his skull. He had always wanted to be enough. It wasn't as Lucy suggested—that he avoided confrontation. No. He simply wanted someone to value him enough that he didn't have to strive for recognition.

Only now the someone had a name—Lucy Hall. He wanted her to care enough about him that she didn't need a reason, no flowers, though he had no objection to that, no need for protection though he would gladly provide it.

He intended to protect her from Smitty should the need arise, even though Lucy quite certainly would say all this hiding and secrecy was only to protect

Roy. She'd insist she could take care of herself. He chuckled.

She backed away and darted him a look. "What's so funny?"

He shrugged. "Everything about us. We enjoy each other's company, don't we?"

Her cheeks captured the heat of the afternoon in a flush of pink. She ducked her head. "I guess so." Then the Lucy he knew pulled herself tall, faced him straight on. "Yes. We do."

He glowed with victory at her confession and wondered if his face turned as pink as hers. "Yet we—" He jerked around at the sound of a horse approaching at a furious pace. Smitty? Had he found them? "Where's Roy?"

"At the tree house, I think."

He grabbed her arm and rushed her to her bedroom. "Stay here and don't come out until I say it's safe." He pulled the door closed and turned around.

To her credit she didn't argue but called through the door. "Be careful. Don't take any chances."

He stalled halfway through a stride. Her concern had been for him. She cared about him. He tucked the knowledge away in the back corner of his thoughts, grabbed the rifle off the wall and ran out the door. A glimpse to the trees. Roy safe in the tree house. "Stay there and be quiet." He strained toward the approaching rider. The horse was familiar. The rider, too. Scout? "What's wrong?" The man couldn't hear above the thudding of the hooves.

Wade raced to meet him, grabbing the halter to stop the horse as Scout jerked back on the reins. His mount was lathered, sides heaving. He'd been rode hard. "What's wrong?"

Scout swung his leg over the horse and ignoring the stirrups, landed on both feet with the strength and vigor of a younger man. No one would guess he was on the verge of death just a few short weeks ago.

"Where's Roy?" He didn't wait for an answer. "Roy," he bellowed.

Roy slid down the tree so fast Wade suspected he would have skid marks on his palms. He galloped to Scout's side. "I'm here."

Scout squatted and grabbed Roy by both shoulders, shaking him gently as if to assure himself he was in one piece. "Good boy."

"Scout?" Something had sent this man into a frenzied ride. Wade wanted to know what.

Scout ran his glance over Roy and scrubbed his hand across the boy's hair. Finally satisfied, he straightened and faced Wade. "Miz Styles at the mercantile says some men have been snooping around asking after a young woman and a ten-year-old boy named Roy."

Wade's insides exploded in hot fury. He'd been so busy thinking of a future with Lucy he'd plumb forgot the present dangers. "Smitty?"

"Can't say, having never met the man but Miz Styles said the one man was big with a mean look—"

Roy made a rude noise in the back of his throat. "That's Smitty, for sure. And probably Louie."

"I expect they've figured out where you are." Scout glanced at Wade. "Let's get this young 'un to safety." He nodded toward his horse, signaling Wade to bring him along. "I thought we could hide him back in the hills or—"

Wade didn't move. "Haven't you forgotten something?"

Scout continued on. "Hurry up, Wade. Who knows how much time we have."

"Scout, Roy isn't the only one needing to be protected from these men. You have a daughter who is equally at risk."

Scout ground to a halt. Slowly, he turned around. "I guess I forgot about her."

A sharp gasp drew their attention to Lucy standing on the step. Her eyes were wide and as dark as a thunderstorm. Her skin had lost all the pretty color of a few minutes ago. She must have heard every word.

Wade dropped the reins and took a step toward her. "Lucy—" He wanted to provide an acceptable reason for Scout's forgetfulness but what excuse could he have? The man thought of Roy but forgot his own flesh and blood. Wade recalled all the times he wondered if Lucy's perceptions were from misunderstood childhood hurts.

This proved they weren't.

He hurt clear through at all her years of pain. No wonder she was so cautious around Scout.

Lucy held up a hand. "Doesn't matter. I'm used to it. This is the way it's always been. I don't exist in his mind."

Scout shuffled his feet, glanced over his shoulder as if expecting Smitty and Louie at any moment. "It was only a mistake," he mumbled.

"Guess that makes me a mistake." She turned and stepped inside, closing the door quietly behind her.

Wade scrubbed at his chin. He wanted to hurry in and assure her she was no mistake. She was perfect in every way and especially perfect for him.

Scout jerked at the reins. "No time to deal with this right now. We have to be prepared for those men."

"Right. Do you have a plan?"

"I was going to hide Roy." He didn't go on. Plainly the man had no real plan.

"Look after your horse then come to the house," Wade said. "We'll discuss plans with Lucy."

"And me," Roy said.

Wade smiled. "For sure. This concerns you, too." He headed for the house as Scout turned toward the barn. What could he say to erase Scout's thoughtlessness? *Lord, show me if there's a way I can help her.*

He opened the door and stepped inside. He didn't see Lucy and called her name.

"I'll be right there." She called from her bedroom, and emerged a few minutes later, her eyes clear, her head held high. If she'd been crying she showed no evidence.

He sensed her fierce pride—protection against Scout's neglect. "I'm sorry."

She quirked her eyebrows. "Why? What did you do?"

"I'm sorry you heard that. It must hurt."

She wilted. "I wish I could say it doesn't. You'd think after all these years...." She didn't finish. Didn't need to. "So it looks like Smitty caught up to us."

"The man needs to be locked up." He couldn't understand why such a villain wandered free while good people ran for their lives. "Let's ask God to protect us."

"I'd like that. I don't mind admitting I'm a little scared."

He met her halfway across the floor and took her hands. They bowed their heads and he prayed aloud. "Our heavenly Father, we need Your protection today as we do every day but more so with Smitty looking for Lucy and Roy. Give us wisdom to outsmart the man." He paused. He wanted to ask the Lord for something more. "Please heal Lucy's hurt. Amen." He opened his eyes.

She kept her head down. Her fingers squeezed his.

Holding on. Taking something from him. Something he freely offered—his protection, his care. His love. He sucked back air. He would do everything he could to end this Smitty threat. Anything he could to help her get past the way Scout treated her.

For a moment, anger surged through his thoughts. How could Scout be so unfeeling? He intended to get an answer from the man. But first, they had to deal with Smitty.

Scout and Roy burst through the door. Lucy slipped her hands from Wade's and stepped back. He wanted to pull her to his side, hold her close but he sensed she wasn't ready to let anyone past her boundaries after what Scout had done.

Roy rushed to Lucy's side. "Smitty caught up to us."

She cupped his shoulder and smiled. "I know. But we'll be fine. So what's the plan?" The smile she gave Wade filled him with pride. She was willing to trust him, accept his help, admit she needed him.

Scout spoke. "You could hide somewhere." His gaze shifted to the trapdoor. "Maybe down there."

"Likely be the first place they look." Wade considered the idea. "Unless we throw a rug over it."

Roy stood in the midst of them, his fists clenched. "I ain't going be locked up. I was before. Didn't care for it."

The three adults stared at him in surprise. Wade glanced at Lucy, saw her concern. He spared Scout a quick look, saw concern and something more—perhaps sorrow?

Wade was sure all three adults were consumed with curiosity and sadness at Roy's announcement but it was Lucy who knelt before him.

"Roy, what happened?"

"It was a long time ago. Before Mr. Peterson took me. Some mean man locked me up at night to keep me from running away."

A moment of silence followed his explanation.

"I guess the cellar is out," Scout said for them all.

Lucy grabbed Roy's hand and they faced Scout and Wade as a team. "I'm through with running. Let Smitty come. We'll be ready."

Tough talk, Wade thought. "What if Smitty waits until we aren't ready?"

"Smitty isn't all that smart. He's just big and mean."

Wade wished he could believe Lucy but he'd met big mean men before and they had a cunning that defied reason.

"We need a plan." Unfortunately, nothing came to mind. There was no place to hide. Running would be futile. Smitty would just follow. He could give Lucy a pistol to carry but would she be able to shoot a man if necessary? It wasn't as easy as it sounded. He'd never been able to do it even though he'd felt the need a time or two.

He slowly turned full circle, considering all his options then came to a halt facing the other three, their gazes on him, waiting, expecting perhaps some sort of solution.

He found none. Mentally, he explored the options—the loft perhaps? Too obvious. The barn? Again, too obvious. "Seems the best thing is to be prepared and confront them."

Lucy nodded. "My idea exactly. I'm not going to spend the rest of my life looking over my shoulder, afraid to go out in public."

Brave words. He admired her spirit but until Smitty was put away for good they would all live in fear.

"Hello the house. Anyone home?" A voice called from a distance away.

Roy jumped like he'd been attacked by the horns of an angry cow.

Lucy pressed her hand to her mouth, her eyes wide.

Scout reached for Roy and pulled him to his side.

Wade scowled at the man. Still worried more about Roy than his own daughter. "Don't think Smitty would be announcing himself like that. You all wait here while I have a look." He cradled the rifle in his arm ready for use and went to the door. A hundred yards down the trail a man sat on his horse waiting to be welcomed or not. "It's an old man."

The rider coughed fit to choke an ox. When he could speak he gasped, "Could you spare me a drink of water?"

Wade lowered the rifle. "Pump's over there."

The man rode wearily to the well, dropped to the ground as if it required his last ounce of energy. It seemed to take all he had to pump some water. He drank heartily then filled his canteen. "Much obliged."

"Where you from?"

The man wiped his arm across his forehead. "Heading for Canada. Heard there's places where the air is so clear it's like a mirror. I figure to get me some rest. Maybe get over this lung problem."

Wade felt Lucy crowding in behind him. "Poor man looks about spent. Could you use some victuals?" she called.

Wade struggled between sympathy for the weariness of the man and caution about inviting strangers into the house.

"We are instructed to entertain strangers," she murmured in his ear.

Remembering when she'd applied the admonition to herself and the delightful afternoon that followed, Wade relented. "You're welcome to come in."

"I thank you." The man left his horse at the corral fence and fair dragged himself to the house.

Lucy sliced bread thick, spread a generous amount of bacon fat on the slices and filled a cup with water.

There were molasses cookies and she set the jar on the table, then stood back as the man sank to the chair.

"May you be rewarded for your kindness," he murmured before he tackled the food.

They stood back watching him. Wade figured the old man was harmless but his nerves twitched knowing not all strangers were so.

The man had another coughing spell. He drained the cup of water and still gasped. He held the cup out to Lucy. "Ma'am, I could sure use another drink."

"Of course." She stepped forward to take the cup.

With the slickness of a snake, he grabbed her wrist and leapt to his feet, all evidence of his weakened state gone. Before Wade could react, the man twisted Lucy's arm and yanked her against his chest. He pulled a gun from under his shirt and pressed it to Lucy's ear.

Wade growled as he surged forward.

Scout grabbed Roy and pulled back toward the stove.

"Hold it. Anyone move and she dies." The kindly old man had turned into a vicious thug.

Wade ground to a halt, his insides roaring with anger.

The man leered at Lucy, setting Wade's heart on fire. "Who are you?" she whispered.

"John Smith. Guess you know my brother,

Eldon Smith, though you might better know him as Smitty."

Lucy gasped.

John Smith chuckled, a sound as menacing as a growl. "I told him we'd get you and that kid and then no one could say he acted other than in self-defense."

"He killed the man in cold blood. He's a coward." Lucy's voice rang with loathing and disgust.

"Lucy." Wade wanted to caution her to guard her words.

Smith jerked her arm hard making her groan. "You're in no position to be sneering."

Wade forced himself to remain still. He needed to think. Figure out how to deal with Smith. The man edged toward the door, keeping Lucy pressed to his chest. Wade eased after them.

"Hold it, mister."

Wade ground to a halt as Smith pressed the gun to Lucy's temple hard enough to make her wince. Her pain shafted through him like a double-edged sword.

Smith reached the door and kicked on it. "Come on, little brother."

Smirking, Smitty strode into the room, a pistol in his hand. He looked around. "Nice job, Johnny boy. Very convincing old man." He squinted toward Scout. "Send the boy over here."

Scout shook his head. "He's just a kid. Leave him be."

Smitty grunted. "Ain't leaving no kid to spread lies about me."

Roy started to sputter. Scout silenced him with a touch.

Wade's mind raced. The odds were stacked against them but he would not let this pair take Lucy one step farther. What he needed was a diversion. *Lord, help us.*

He held Lucy's gaze sending silent messages of assurance. Hoping she read his love, his promise to stop these men. Her eyelids flickered. She darted her gaze to one side, widened her eyes and looked expectant.

What was she trying to tell him?

Again her gaze jerked to his right, down toward his feet then returned, eyes wide and demanding.

He didn't move but slowly shifted his eyes to the spot she indicated. A length of yarn went from the chair leg beside him. It was taut, leading toward Lucy's room.

He met her gaze again, saw that this was what she wanted him to see. Silently, slowly, cautiously he shifted his gaze toward Scout and tipped his eyeballs toward the yarn. Scout saw the yarn and indicated with a flick of his eyelids that he saw it.

Wade hesitated. He didn't know what Lucy had in

mind but he knew when he moved all of them would be in danger.

"Give me the kid." Smitty reached past his brother.

Now was the time to act. He caught his boot on the yarn and kicked. A great clatter sounded in the bedroom and both the Smiths jerked their attention toward the noise.

It was all the distraction Wade needed. He leapt across the room and caught Lucy who had used the moment to escape her captor.

Wade grabbed the rifle where he'd left it when he invited the "old" man in and ducked out the door all in one movement.

He'd caught a glimpse of Scout moving, hoped he managed to relieve Smitty of his gun.

The Smiths roared in unison, a sound that tingled the skin on the back of Wade's neck and made Lucy tremble. He pulled her close. "I've got you." The way she held on, he wondered if she didn't have him.

They pressed to the warm boards of the wall and edged along the wall. A gunshot rang out.

Lucy gasped.

They reached the window and Wade eased over the ledge to have a look. He couldn't see well enough and pressed closer.

Just then, Lucy gave him an almighty shove tumbling him clean off the stoop. A shot rang out. Then another.

"Lucy," he roared as he rolled to his stomach and bolted to his feet. "Lucy."

She lay faceup on the stoop.

Both Smith men came from the door, Scout holding the men's own pistols at their backs.

Wade rushed to Lucy's side, bent over, afraid to touch her. He skimmed his gaze over her body, saw no blood. "Lucy." The word tore flesh from his throat as he forced it out.

She groaned. "Help me sit up."

He sat because his legs had gone weak as butter and pulled her up facing him. "Are you hurt?"

Leaning forward, she gasped for air. "Knocked my breath out." She blinked and rubbed the back of her head. "Oww."

Relief left him weak, then surged through him in waves of foreign emotion. "Why did you push me? Were you trying to kill me?"

Scout chuckled. "Think she might have saved your life. This old codger was all set to shoot you. Good thing he ain't too quick or he might have hit something besides the roof."

Wade glanced up and saw the bullet hole over his head. That would be the first shot he heard.

"Good thing I was quick enough to get Smitty's gun. I stopped him from getting off another shot."

"You shot my hand." Smith groaned in pain but Wade felt no sympathy.

He turned to Lucy. "You fool woman. You might have been killed."

Her grin was very wobbly. "It never crossed my mind. I only thought of him shooting you."

His insides melted. Her only concern had been for him. She cared about him. His nose stung, his throat tightened. His heart pounding against his ribs, he pulled her into his arms.

"Save that for later," Scout growled. "I could use some help getting this pair into town."

"Riders coming," Roy called from inside the house.

Wade sighed. "Used to be a quiet little ranch."

Lucy giggled. "You mean before I came?"

He allowed himself to run his hand over her hair and along her cheek, all the time looking deep into eyes as gray as morning fog across the plains. He kissed her sweet little nose then pulled her to her feet. "Guess I better see who it is."

He rescued the rifle and strode around the corner of the house. "It's the marshal and some men," he called to the others. When the knot of men reined to a halt before him, the marshal nodded. "You happen to see a couple of strangers around here? Smith by name?"

"As a matter of fact…" He indicated over his shoulder.

"Everything all right?" the marshal asked.

Wade grinned. "We're all safe."

"I'll take those two off your hands." He signaled a couple of the riders who dismounted and roughly grabbed the Smiths.

The marshal dismounted slowly. "Care to tell me what happened here?"

"We'll be glad to," Wade said. And then he could turn his attention back to Lucy—his sweet, brave Lucy.

Chapter Thirteen

Lucy wanted to make coffee and serve the marshal as he sat at the table but every time she stood, her legs buckled.

Wade pressed his hand to her shoulder. "Sit. I'll make coffee."

"I doubt your statement will be needed but just in case...." The marshal signaled for paper and pencil from one of the many deputies. "Seems his accomplice, Louie, was getting nervous. Hinted to the sheriff he might have valuable information in exchange for an easy sentence. And then he was shot. Smitty didn't know there was a witness which is why he was after the two of you, wanting to make sure there was no one alive to testify against him."

Her hand unsteady, Lucy wrote out a statement of what she'd seen. Roy insisted he would do so as well.

Then the marshal wanted to know how they had captured the pair.

Wade laughed, his gaze warm and admiring as he told of the yarn Lucy had fastened to the table leg. "What made you think to do that?"

She shrugged. "I only wanted a way to signal you if they showed up and I couldn't get to the triangle. I didn't intend to let them take me without a fight."

"It saved all our hides."

"You sound like a spunky woman," the marshal said. "We could use the likes of you in the country." He folded the finished papers and tucked them into the inside pocket of his vest. "I think that will be the last you hear of them."

He left with his posse, the Smiths securely escorted.

Wade, Scout and Lucy sat at the table sagging with relief.

"Glad that's over," Wade said. He ached inside and out. He wondered if his heart would ever stop rattling against his ribs.

"Can I go out to the tree house?" Roy asked.

The three waved him away.

Lucy sighed. "Wish I had the energy to run and play."

"How's your head?"

She rubbed it gingerly. "It's fine. The emotional stuff has left me drained though. You know, being so scared and so..." She shrugged.

He guessed from the way she avoided looking at Scout that she meant the words she'd overheard. Seems from what was said then and probably on other occasions that the words and deeds had built brick after brick. No wonder Lucy had such thick walls around her heart.

And he didn't want them there. He wanted nothing separating him from her caring spirit he had glimpsed in the way she dealt with Roy, the way she laughed at life and especially—his heart picked up pace again—the way she had so readily risked her life for him.

Seems it was time to probe the wound and pull out the festering thorn. "Scout." He gave the man a steady, no-punches-pulled look. "You plumb forgot Lucy when you came from town."

Scout stared at his hands hanging between his knees. "It was a mistake," he mumbled.

Lucy's hands clenched together. "Leave it, Wade. You can't change history."

Wade shook his head. "At the very least you deserve an explanation." He stared hard enough at Scout to light a fire on the top of his head, which was all he could see as the man hunched over his lap. "Scout, is Lucy right? Do you consider her a mistake?"

The man didn't move and the silence hung between them like a dirty, smelly rag.

"Don't you think she deserves more of an explanation than you made a mistake?"

Still no response and Wade waited, determined the man would give Lucy some sort of answer. Then Scout shuddered. "It was her mother's fault."

"Tell her. Not me."

Scout shifted so slightly a person could have missed it. As if it hurt him to actually face her. Had he always treated her this way?

Lucy did not want to hear this. He'd provide excuses which would only make her feel worse, not better. The past was done. She wished she could cover her ears and block out his words. *Lord, You can make deaf ears hear, please make my hearing ears deaf. Guard my heart from the hurt he'll give.*

Scout continued, totally unaware she didn't want to hear anything he had to say. "That woman was always pushing at me. Wanting things I couldn't give her. She used to be a wild as…." He shrugged as if he didn't want to remember or perhaps didn't want to tell Lucy the truth.

"She always said she had a life before Christ that she wasn't proud of."

He nodded. "She wanted to get married. Figured if she tricked me into making a baby with her, I would. That's how you was born."

"So, I was a mistake. At least Mama had the decency not to tell me so." She couldn't keep the bitter note from her voice and when Wade reached across the table for her hands, she pulled them to her lap. She needed no one's pity. She'd faced the shame of being born out of wedlock long ago. "Good thing God sees me with eyes of love not condemnation or regret." There were times she'd doubted that, but lately she had grown more certain of it.

"It wasn't because of you exactly," Scout murmured, still not able to look at her. "I just wasn't ready to settle down. I wasn't ready to be a husband, let alone a father."

Lucy said nothing. No need to tell her that. He'd made it as plain as the dirt on which they walked every day.

"Then one day I realized I was."

"Was what?"

"Ready to be a husband and father. I found this place. Built this house. Even got myself some cows." He looked at Wade who watched them with a certain caution as if he wondered at the tension between them.

She would never be able to adequately explain how it felt to wonder if her father even saw her, and now to have it confirmed that he considered her a mistake… well, it burned all the way down her insides until it stung the soles of her feet.

Scout sighed. "Then I heard that Margaret had died. I realized I'd waited too long to get myself ready."

"You never came to the funeral."

"'Twas too late when I heard and I couldn't face my failures. Seems I've built my life on them."

She stared at her father. He had regrets?

"I guess I mourned Margaret for about six months then I realized my plans didn't have to end. I had a daughter. I figured I would get you to come and give you the home I never had."

"It was way too late. Besides, why would I even consider the idea? You never saw me when I was a child. Or perhaps—" She thought of his recent words. "Perhaps you saw me as a mistake. Seems you can't look at me, see me any more now than you could when I was growing up."

His head jerked up. "I saw you. I memorized every detail of you. Why, I remember the way your hair hung down in twin braids that flipped against your back when you ran. Seems you ran everywhere."

He sure had a strange way of showing his notice. "You hardly spoke to me. Never even said goodbye when you rode out. Did you know I used to stand with my nose pressed to the window, my tears fogging the glass, wishing, hoping, waiting for you to just once turn around and wave?"

"I had nothing to give you. Just as I had nothing to give your mother. That's why I wanted to get this house and ranch into shape before I sent for her—and you."

Lucy sent a silent appeal to Wade. Hearing her

father confess his feelings of inadequacy, seeing the defeat in his eyes left her floundering for solid ground. How did she deal with this?

Wade smiled so gently, so kindly she felt even further off-kilter.

"I didn't know how to deal with a little girl. Skirts and bonnets and pretty shoes. I couldn't face you because I knew I failed you. I guess it became a habit."

Fury as pure and unfettered as the prairie wind raged through her turning up debris of her past, boulders of the present. "Habit," she spat out the word. "Please don't excuse your neglect as habit. It was hurtful. Still is." She sprang to her feet. "Look at me. Really look at me."

Scout did so.

She felt Wade's surprised stare as well, but she held Scout's gaze in a demanding lock.

"See me. Do I look like you or my mother? Am I plain or pretty?" She closed her eyes. "What color are my eyes?"

She gave him a second to answer and when he didn't, she opened them again and blazed him with a mixture of fury and sorrow. "I'm real. I'm a person. Not a mistake. Pinch me, I hurt. Treat me like I don't exist and I hurt." Her breathing became ragged. "I deserve to be seen and acknowledged." Her anger fled, leaving her weak and teary. She would not let one single tear escape. She would not reveal a bit of weakness.

Letting out a huff of air, she turned and headed toward the stove. She'd cook. That would relieve some tension but she didn't make two steps before Scout caught her hand.

"You have your mother's eyes. They're gray though they darken to almost black when you are angry. Like right now. But you have my chin and my temper. Heaven help us both. I have avoided you because I know how big a failure I am but when I thought Smith had shot you… Well, I realized if I didn't change, it would always be too late for us just like it is for your mother and me."

Lucy stared. "You know you spoke more words to me in that little speech than in my entire life."

His smile was tenuous. "I can't make any promises but perhaps you'd give me a chance to try again?"

She studied him for one full minute, searching for sincerity in his gaze. She thought she found it but she wasn't prepared to throw caution out the door. "I'll try, but I've been disappointed so many times."

"That's all I ask." He pushed to his feet and headed outdoors, his gait slow and measured as if he suddenly felt sick.

She could only hope the realization of how his treatment had hurt her would have some affect on him. Then she remembered Wade and turned to him.

"It's a start," he said. "It's up to both of you to make it work."

She studied him a long time remembering his protective arms around her, how she'd clung to him. From the way heat stole up her neck, she knew her cheeks blazed with color and she ducked away.

He'd cared enough to protect her. He'd cared enough to try and resolve the strain between her and Scout.

He cared. Sure he'd said it already but his actions had more than proved it.

She didn't know where to look. Couldn't meet his eyes. Couldn't let him see how she glowed inside. Couldn't let him guess the reason.

He headed for the door. "I better go check on the horses." He squeezed her shoulder as he left, and he might as well have squeezed her heart the way it blasted blood through her veins.

The feeling around the table as they gathered for supper rang with victory. Smitty would no longer haunt their thoughts. They had all lived through the ordeal. And Lucy had learned some things about Scout she hoped would make it easier for them to be father and daughter.

She felt a bit of strain as she watched him across the table. But when he looked at her of his own accord for the first time in her life, she felt like she was truly his daughter.

She returned his smile then shifted her gaze to Wade. He smiled as if he shared her well-being.

She owed him for helping them to this fragile place. Somehow, she'd find a way to thank him.

Roy gobbled up his food with his usual gusto then shoved from the table and dashed outside before she served dessert.

"Are you sick, Roy?" she called.

He raced back inside with an armload of wildflowers that he placed in her lap. "For you."

"Why, thank you." She buried her nose in the lovely bouquet.

Wade laughed. "You don't waste any time, do you?"

What an odd comment. "What do you mean?" Then she remembered how Roy planned to persuade her to stay here with gifts and burst out laughing.

"Is this a secret joke?" Scout asked, confused why they should laugh at a handful of wildflowers.

Wade and Roy explained Roy's plan.

Lucy kept her face buried in the flowers. There was no reason not to return to Dry Creek now but she didn't want to go. She and Scout were just beginning to discover what they'd never had and then there was Wade. She wanted to see what would happen to this tender feeling between them.

Something had shifted in the last few hours in her feelings for Wade. He cared. She knew it, believed it.

But she wasn't quite sure she was ready to let down all the barriers around her heart.

Next morning, Wade stared out across the corral fence. He had promised to help Scout with the construction of the barn. It would soon be completed. After that he had no reason to stay. But he didn't want to leave. He'd fallen in love with the land. He hadn't thought much about settling down until recently, but now he couldn't imagine continuing his nomad way of life.

He wanted a farm of his own. He thought of the few dollars he'd managed to save and knew he would not be purchasing land. He'd have to homestead. Maybe he'd see if he could find land close to Scout so Lucy and her father could learn to appreciate each other.

Whoa there, cowboy. How had he gone from thinking of being a landowner, to building a home for Lucy?

But that's what he wanted.

He'd fallen in love with Lucy and wanted to make a home and share it with her.

Roy, too. He had no objection to making the boy part of their family.

Wade knew Lucy cared for him. She'd made that plain enough. But whether or not she was ready to trust her heart to the love of another person—specifically Wade Miller—was another question entirely. And the answer might not come immediately.

He caught a glimpse of movement and turned to watch Roy scrounging for more flowers. The boy had the right idea in trying to convince her to stay.

Wade leaned more heavily on his arms. He could bring flowers. But he wanted to show her his love of the land. Create in her a need to share that love, share his love, build a home together.

He thought of his favorite place. "I'll show her that and she'll for sure want to stay."

He wandered into the house to speak to her. Her braid flew as she hurried to the stove to tend a pot.

His mouth dried, his intentions wilted. What if she didn't want to ride to the hill? Didn't want to spend her life with a rancher or—if he must homestead to get land—a farmer? He grabbed a drink of water.

She smiled at him, setting his heart to racing. "Supper will be about an hour. I'll ring the triangle when it's ready."

He carried her smile under his heart as he returned to work. He almost hummed but knowing how the sound affected both man and beast, he contented himself with smiling as he worked on the barn.

Scout had disappeared on some mysterious errand and Roy still picked wildflowers so Wade could enjoy his pleasure privately without anyone commenting on his foolish grin.

The hour seemed like three. He glanced at the

house every few minutes wondering why she didn't ring the triangle. Instead, he watched her dart in and out, tossing water to the grass, draping tea towels over some low bushes and generally flirting with his thoughts.

Knowing she was safe now that Smitty and his brother were guarded by the marshal and several deputies made his pleasure grow.

But wanting to spend every minute with her formed a much larger, more demanding urgency. He tackled a spike, driving it home in bone-shuddering blows. Wouldn't be wise to build dreams as big as this barn until he knew if Lucy gal loved him and shared his hopes for the future.

When the triangle finally clanged, Wade threw down his hammer and, restraining his stride to a quick walk, headed for the house. Scout had returned a few minutes ago and fell in beside him. Roy skipped toward the house, his arms full of flowers.

Lucy fed them another fine meal. Her biscuits and browned gravy certainly filled lots of empty corners in his belly. But as his stomach filled, his heart grew hungrier. He wanted to speak of his feelings. Yet, every time he thought of it he almost choked.

Roy ate six biscuits drowned in gravy before he came up for air. "Lucy's a good cook, ain't she?" He didn't wait for the obvious answer. "I'll bet you wish she could stay here forever."

Wade dare not look at anyone for fear they would

see his longing. But he felt Scout's surprise. The man sucked in air for a full twenty seconds. When he spoke, his voice had a deeper than usual tone. "Sure could use a woman's touch around here," he managed. "Besides, I always figured this would be her home."

Lucy laughed. Wade thought she sounded more surprised than amused. "I'd say more than a touch is needed. Try good old-fashioned lye soap and a generous amount of elbow grease. I practically worked the skin off my fingers scrubbing everything." She held out her hands for inspection. "Look. I'm still wrinkled like a prune."

One glance. Just at her hands. That's all he'd allow himself. If he looked at her laughing eyes, her teasing smile, he feared he'd embarrass them all by blurting out the words blazing across his mind. *Stay, Lucy gal. Stay. Let me marry you and make you a part of my life forever. I know I could make you happy. You sure do make me happy.*

Wade busied himself swiping up the last of the gravy with a bit of biscuit. He sat back and smacked his lips before he raised his eyes to glance at her hands. Despite his decision to limit it to that, his stubborn eyes did what they ached to do—they sought her face.

She smiled at him. Teasing? Maybe. But maybe something more. Something that flooded his heart with hope. "Lucy gal—" He stopped his mouth before the secret words erupted.

She watched, waiting for him to finish.

He swallowed hard, grabbed his glass and downed water like he'd stepped from the heat of a burning building. *Say something, man. Don't act like such a dolt.* "Lucy gal, I promised I'd show you the big hill. I'll saddle the horses and take you there this evening." There, he'd managed to say the words without making a fool of himself.

Her eyes flashed. She smiled. "I'd like that."

He hoped his grin was the only outward sign he gave of how happy her agreement made him.

"I'll have to do dishes first."

He'd always hated doing dishes but it suddenly seemed like the best job in the world. "I'll help."

She produced a pudding for dessert.

Roy spoke for all of them as he gobbled his down. "This tastes real good. Is it all gone?"

Lucy laughed. "One thing about you, Roy. You never complain about food of any sort. You'll be glad to know I saved the pot for you to clean out."

Roy rushed to the cupboard and tackled the job.

Wade grinned at Lucy. "You probably won't have to wash it when he's done." His heart forgot to beat as Lucy's amused gaze caught his. It took every ounce of inner strength to turn away before he did something foolish like blurt out his deepest desire—to be able to show her his love for the rest of their lives.

Roy ran his finger around the pot one more time and licked off every bit of flavor. "I guess there ain't no more."

Scout scraped his chair back. "Soon as you're done there, young Roy, we'll go see if we can scare up some meat."

Roy immediately brightened. "I'm done already." He hurried to the stoop and waited.

Scout took the rifle from its mount. Lucy gathered up a handful of dishes. Scout paused at her side. He seemed to search for what he wanted to say.

Lucy waited, keeping her gaze on the plates she held.

"Lucy, your ma would be proud to see how you've grown up." And then he was gone.

Lucy stood motionless until the clatter of boots died away and then sighed and headed to the stoop and the dishpan.

Did she find Scout's faint approval satisfying or hurtful? Wade could guess until the cows came home but only Lucy knew. He followed her to the stoop, his arms full of dirty dishes. He snagged a towel off the bushes and dried as she washed.

He felt her tension, knew to mention it would likely make it worse. A person needed time to gather up hurt and disappointment and put it into perspective. He waited for her to break the silence if she so chose. He didn't mind if they talked or not, her company was enough for him.

He dried the dishes as she washed then flipped the towel back to the bush to dry. "I'll get the horses."

As he saddled Two Bit and a reluctant Queenie, he prayed. For healing the rift between Lucy and her pa, for wisdom and patience to let God do His work. God knew better than he how much she needed to sort this out so she could learn to trust another man—not just any man, of course. Only him.

He led the horses back to the stoop where she waited. She looked so pretty in her brown cotton dress. His heart kicked into a gallop as he led her toward Queenie, her hand in his—cool and soft. He caught her around the waist and half lifted her into the saddle. For a heartbeat he considered forgetting about the horse, the saddle, even the ride, wanting to pull her into his arms instead. Thankfully, his arms obeyed his head rather than his heart and he released her as she settled and took up Queenie's reins.

He promised himself he would be sure to lift her down when they got home. And if she happened to tumble into his arms it wouldn't be his fault. He'd find it unobjectionable in every way.

He swung onto Two Bit's back and, ignoring the way his horse tossed his head in protest, kept him to a pace that matched Queenie's lumbering gait so he could ride at Lucy's side. His heart flooded with feelings and longings for which he could not find words. Probably a good thing. Instead, he spoke of the things he found familiar and safe.

"The grass here looks dried but it's full of nutrition. Cows do well on it."

"Seems so dry. Where do the animals get water?"

"The creek, plus there are several springs that Scout dug out so we get a nice flow."

She looked about in interest. "Lots of wildflowers."

He hadn't paid any attention before being mostly interested in grass and game but now he looked and sure enough, bits of color dotted the prairie.

She pointed out every new type she saw.

Seeing her pleasure filled him with such sweetness he felt like he breathed in honey.

They didn't take a direct route to their destination. He wanted her to see everything, but eventually he angled toward the highest point on the ranch.

"You can't tell we're climbing, can you?"

She laughed. "Queenie makes every step feel like she's scaling a mountain."

"She's rough all right. Do you want me to ride her?"

"Oh, I'm not uncomfortable. I only meant she acts like such a martyr, but thanks for offering." The look she gave him made the sun seem more golden.

He guessed he looked as pleased as Roy did leaving with Scout and turned his attention to the scenery.

A few minutes later they reached the crest of the

hill. A rocky butte stood at the very top and he reined in there. He jumped down and before she could make a move to dismount, he lifted her from the saddle. She stood inches from him, her face turned down as she brushed her skirts. He waited, wanting to see more than the top of her head. Probably surprised that he remained so close, she pulled her gaze to him, her eyes round with mysterious depths. Her lips parted as if she meant to speak and then she closed her mouth and stepped back. "So, this is the place?"

He reined his thoughts into order. "This is it."

She looked. "You're right. You can see for miles."

"You ain't seen nothing yet."

He reached for her hand, pleased when she allowed him to take it without protest.

She laughed as he pulled her past the rocks. Twenty feet farther the view opened up like someone had cut it with a can opener.

She gasped and squeezed his hand. "Oh, my."

Her reaction filled him with pride as if he owned the view. He let her drink in the sight for several minutes without saying anything then he pointed. "Look, you can see Lark."

She squinted. "Where?"

"Follow the horizon from right to left until you see a little rise."

She shook her head in frustration. "I can't see."

"Here." He pulled her in front of him and pressed

her to his chest so he could put his head close to hers. His senses flooded with her nearness and he suddenly couldn't speak. She smelled like the warm prairie, a mixture of sweet and spice. From the first time he saw her he'd wanted to touch her hair and assess it's silkiness. He'd touched it several times but still hadn't satisfied his curiosity.

Her braid hung down her back and he picked it up and lifted it over her shoulder. Its weight surprised him and its texture—silkier than anything he'd ever felt. The only thing that he could think that seemed close was the tender petals on the wild roses.

"I still can't see it."

Her words pulled him back to the reason he held her in his arms. He rested one hand on her shoulder, and with the other pointed toward Lark. She followed his finger. "Lower. Just above the horizon."

"I see it." She grabbed his pointing hand and squeezed. "How far is it?"

"I estimate it to be fifteen or twenty miles."

"I feel like I can see forever."

He turned her slightly. "What do you see over there?" He touched her chin with his free hand and turned her face. Telling himself he needed to make sure she focused in the correct direction, he kept his fingers on her chin. It took more self-control than he knew he was capable of to resist turning her into his arms.

"What am I looking for?"

"The ranch." He hoped she couldn't hear the husky longing in his voice.

"Is that it?" She pointed but continued to hold his hand.

"That's it."

"Look. Isn't that Pa and Roy?"

He saw the pair, no bigger than ants, heading toward a dark spot he knew to be some bushes. "Looking for prairie chicken."

She slipped from his arms and sat a few feet away.

He waited for his disappointment to seep out in degrees, then sat down keeping a generous four inches between them. He wanted less but guessed she would want more.

"Lucy, you like the prairies, don't you?"

"They're beautiful."

"Would you want to live here?"

She turned slowly to stare at him. "You're sounding like Roy."

"Roy wants you to stay."

"I guess so."

God help me find the words. Help me not to rush her and scare her off.

"Well, cowboy, exactly what do you have in mind?" Her voice deepened, vibrating across his senses. The look she gave him searched deep into his soul, seeking something she could trust. He met her look with quiet confidence. What he offered would never change, never falter; he'd never forget a promise spoken or unspoken. He loved her and he wanted her to know it, trust it.

"Lucy, you must know how I feel about you. I love you. I want to share my life with you."

Her eyes flared. He let himself think she welcomed the idea. Then her gaze drifted toward the ranch and her shoulders crept toward her ears.

He couldn't guess what troubled her.

He slid closer until they sat shoulder to shoulder. "Lucy, remember when you said I ran from life or hid from it, letting people say things about me but not caring. I cared. But it seemed no one ever saw me as anything but a convenience or inconvenience. They didn't see me as me."

She took his hand, her touch robbing those feelings of their power. "I see you as more than a convenience." She giggled. "Or even an inconvenience." She turned and smiled at him, the glow of the descending sun catching her in her eyes, filling his heart with gold.

"I know you do."

"But—"

"I hate buts."

She nodded, her expression regretful. "I feel like I've just been thrown into the rushing waters of a deep river. Scout's words, Smitty's capture…well, my thoughts are in such a turmoil I don't even know what I think."

"Of course." He had to be patient. Give her time to see that he would never treat her with the same carelessness Scout had. "Promise me you'll think about it."

She still held his hand and squeezed it. "I promise."

Chapter Fourteen

Think about Wade's proposal? She didn't need to promise. In the days that followed, his words filled every space in Lucy's thoughts to the exclusion of all else.

Roy had almost every can and jug in the house full of flowers. "You'll erase every trace of wildflowers from the country if you keep it up," she'd warned him a few days ago and made him promise to pick only one bouquet a week.

She knew how badly he wanted to stay. This was the first bit of family he'd ever enjoyed. Of course he wanted to stay.

Did she?

Wade loved her.

She loved him.

The admission sang through her like the voice of a thousand angels.

But he'd said nothing about where he wanted to live. Did he think to live here with Scout? She wasn't sure she wanted that. Yes, Scout had made an effort to mend the rift between them but her feelings were still new and raw concerning him. Perhaps they would never be what they should be or could have been.

If Wade were to suggest a place of their own...

Was she ready to trust her whole life into the hands of a man after her disappointment with Scout?

Everything was so confusing.

She ducked into her bedroom and opened her Bible. *Lord, speak to me.* She turned to Psalm one hundred and eighteen where she had found direction only a few days ago. She read the entire chapter but the only words that seemed especially directed to her were those in verse eight, *It is better to trust in the Lord than to put confidence in man.*

It wasn't what she wanted to hear even though she had lived most of her life by those words.

She stared out the window. The words didn't give peace because they didn't reach the truth deep in her heart.

She loved Wade. She wanted to feel confident to share his life.

Lord, give me a sign that I can trust my heart to him.

God had been with her all her life, her friend and guide. She would wait for Him to answer that prayer.

* * *

A day passed. Two. She tried to ignore her impatience. She watched and listened carefully, looking for a sign from God. But the sky seemed empty.

She stood on the step, the damp tea towel in her hands and looked about. It was a pleasant place. She'd grown fond of it. The kitchen bore the mark of her hard work. Meals were satisfying to make. She enjoyed letting her gaze wander across the landscape, zeroing in on tiny details. The creek offered a pleasant retreat throughout the day.

But she didn't want to be the housekeeper. The cook. Nor only Scout's daughter.

She wanted a life of her own—shared with Wade.

God, I'm waiting for a sign. But I confess I am impatient.

The sound of hammering drew her attention to a spot behind the corrals where Scout and Roy were busy. *I wonder what they're up to.* Then she turned to put things away.

Over supper, Roy gobbled his food with more haste than usual. "What's your hurry?" Lucy asked.

He stopped and made an effort to slow down. Still, he finished well before the rest of them and refused seconds. "Are you almost done?" he asked Scout.

Pa swirled gravy through his potatoes and arranged them into a tidy circle seemingly oblivious to Roy's impatience.

Lucy ducked her head to hide her smile. He must have promised to take Roy hunting for him to be so impatient.

Slowly Scout ate his potatoes, took his time at picking each morsel from his plate while Roy fidgeted and sighed.

Finally, Scout pushed his plate away. "Guess I'm done."

"Now?" Roy asked, almost bouncing from his chair.

Scout nodded. "Now."

Roy rushed to Lucy and grabbed her hand. "We got a surprise for you. Come on."

"Me?" This excitement was on her behalf? She shot Scout a look. He grinned at her just as she'd always dreamed he would, which only served to further confuse her. She wasn't sure how to deal with a father who actually saw her.

"Come on." Roy dragged her toward the door.

Scout followed looking as pleased as all get-out.

"You coming?" she asked Wade, suddenly afraid to face this alone.

He sprang to his feet. "Wouldn't miss it for the world."

She could barely keep up with Roy as he pulled her across the yard. Behind the corrals a high chicken-wire fence created a yard around the small building. Did she hear the murmur of hens?

They drew to a halt at the wood-framed gate. "See

how you open it." Roy unhooked the wire and shepherded her inside. He rushed over and threw open the door and four hens rushed out clucking.

"Chickens?" She sounded as surprised as she felt.

"I asked around and the Perrys said they could spare a few." He reached inside the building, pulled out a wire basket and handed it to Lucy.

"Four eggs."

"Mrs. Perry says they're good layers." He touched her elbow. "Look inside."

She did so and saw a little pen with a clucking hen.

"She's setting a dozen eggs. You could have a nice-sized flock in another year."

Lucy stared at the hen. Slowly shifted her gaze to stare at Scout. "Next year? You're wanting me to stay?"

A wary look came to his eyes. "They're yours, Lucy. Wherever you go, you take them."

She understood his caution and something inside her fortressed heart cracked open. "Thanks. I'll get some food for them." She took the eggs to the house and returned with a bucket full of kitchen scraps.

They watched the hens dive after the food as if the whole thing was worth charging admission.

"I better do the dishes," she said finally.

Next day, her afternoon chores complete, Lucy paced the floor pausing to look out the window.

She went to the porch and studied the yard. The hens clucked and scratched inside their pen. It still amazed her that Scout had brought her chickens—an unusual gift. And perhaps that's why it confused her. What did he intend it to mean?

Never mind. Eggs were more than welcome. She grabbed the pan of scraps she'd saved and headed out to the new chicken house.

She made sure the setting hen had food and water then left the pen. The air was so calm and peaceful every sound seemed magnified—from the ducks murmuring on the creek, to the grasshoppers sawing on the grass, to the crow wings combing the air overhead.

In fact, she could pinpoint where Scout and Wade were. There'd been hammering a few minutes ago but now she heard their voices and could make out each word.

Scout was saying something about the ranch. She didn't intentionally eavesdrop, but the warm still air and her uncertain thoughts created a sort of inertia and she didn't have the energy to move. Besides, she couldn't imagine they'd say anything she shouldn't overhear.

"You can have the ranch when I die. In the meantime, I'll make you my partner." Scout's voice came clear as the sky overhead. "It's what I owe you for bringing Lucy. I know you said you would but I never thought you'd succeed."

"That's right generous of you."

Lucy's thoughts skidded to a shocked halt. Wade had come for her simply to get the ranch? What did his words of love mean? Why did he want her to stay? Was it only because the place needed a housekeeper? It had been mentioned often enough but she'd given the suggestion little thought. She didn't want to be a housekeeper. She wanted far more.

She spun away from the fence and rushed for the house.

Oh, God, this is not the sign I wanted but I cannot ignore it.

Her mind whirled with denials and accusations. She should have known better than to follow her foolish heart seeking the approval she'd wanted all her life.

She ran up and down the cellar ladder bringing up things to make—she didn't have any idea what she planned. All she knew was she must work, keep her thoughts locked behind busyness so the hurt wouldn't consume her.

But working at a furious pace didn't shake the awful feeling she was falling through space.

She'd trusted Wade, believed his words. Thought he could give her what Scout hadn't. Whatever that was. She no longer knew.

The house crowded her. She needed space. She knew where she could find it. On the hill where Wade had taken her.

Fleeing her tortured thoughts she slipped out to the corrals. Hammering came from the new barn. They would never notice her riding away on Queenie and she'd be back before they even realized she was gone.

Bitterness colored her thoughts in stark colors. So long as she had the meals ready on time she doubted they'd even notice if she disappeared for hours.

Queenie leaned against the corral fence, one leg lifted. She tossed her head and dug in her hooves at being asked to leave her pleasant nap.

"Don't be difficult. I'm in no mood for it."

The horse pricked up her ears and seemed to jerk to attention.

"Forget the dramatics. You and I are going for a ride. And I'll put up with none of your nonsense today."

The saddle was in the old barn. She didn't want to risk being seen and having anyone demand to know what she was up to in order to get it. "We rode all the way here bareback. I'll do it again." She scowled at Queenie as the horse shied away. "Stop acting up."

Lucy opened the gate and led Queenie out then pulled herself onto the horse's back and kicked her sides.

Queenie snorted a protest but didn't lift one of her four feet.

"Now." Lucy kicked her again and this time she made it plain she meant business. With all the hurt air of a slighted dowager, Queenie plodded across the yard.

Lucy could see the hill in the distance and pointed the horse in that direction. The other day when she and Wade had made this ride, it seemed to take only a few minutes but today Queenie's pace made it take forever.

"Let's hurry it up a bit. I want to be there before snow falls." But her constant urging only made Queenie more uncooperative. "I wouldn't have believed it possible for you to get any worse. What is the matter with you?"

But finally they started to climb.

Another reason for Queenie to complain. She snuffled and grunted.

"Stop whining. We're almost there." Lucy didn't know who was more relieved when they reached the top. She dropped to the ground and looked about for something to secure Queenie's halter to. The best she could do was a low bush. But Queenie wasn't likely to run off. It took too much effort.

Lucy returned to the place where she and Wade had sat and settled herself. She studied the landscape spread out before her. So peaceful. So serene.

Why couldn't she feel as calm?

Why had God sent her here? Yes, she and Scout had perhaps mended some broken areas, though she wasn't about to throw herself unreservedly into the relationship.

It was a good place for Roy. No reason he couldn't stay.

She knew she skirted the thing that bothered her most.

Her feelings for Wade.

Why had she allowed herself to fall in love with him?

The verse the Lord had given her blazoned across her mind and she spoke the words aloud. "It is better to trust in the Lord than to put confidence in man." She'd certainly learned the truth of those words.

Why, God? Why?

Why did the men she cared about always let her down? Why couldn't she find one who would value her for herself and not see her as either a mistake or a means to an end?

Remembering how Wade thought of himself as a convenience or an inconvenience, she sniffed. They were more alike in this regard than she cared to admit.

How had she responded to his admission?

By assuring him she saw him as neither. What did she see him as?

After overhearing the words indicating she was only a way to get the ranch, she no longer knew.

Wade. Scout. The pair twisted through her thoughts.

And hens. Why had Scout given her hens? Did

he hope to convince her to stay? Did he want her to? Would she if he did?

How could she trust any of them?

It is better to trust in the Lord than to put confidence in man.

She sighed. Yes, she could trust God but sometimes she felt like Roy. She wanted someone with a face and arms right here on earth to trust.

Better to trust in the Lord.

Better? Better. An idea budded. Of course trusting God was better. But—the idea slowly unfolded as if touched by unseen hands—that didn't mean it was wrong, or foolish, or impossible to trust man.

She thought of how she held up a yardstick for Scout, wanting, needing to make him measure up. How he fell short of the mark.

And now she was doing the same to Wade. Judging a conversation she'd overheard without asking for an explanation.

Perhaps she only needed to trust man as imperfect. Not unkind. Not unfaithful. Just not able to measure up to the impossible expectations she had.

Only God would never disappoint.

If she wanted love and relationship, family and belonging here on earth she had to accept it from people who would make mistakes.

She contemplated the idea a bit longer, asking God to insert things into her mind to help her sort out her discovery. The whole idea grew defined. Clear. She could trust those close to her but ultimately, they would fail. Only God would never let her down. She thought of a verse her ma had often quoted. Couldn't say where it was in the Bible. *God will not fail thee nor forsake thee.*

She'd give Scout another chance accepting that he would sometimes fail, sometimes disappoint but whatever he offered her was worth taking.

She'd ask Wade to explain the conversation. And she'd tell him she loved him. And if he still loved her, accepted her with her flaws…well, perhaps they could start anew and with her new willingness to accept an imperfect love, they might do all right.

Lord, is this what you've been trying to tell me? Is this why You brought me here? To show me this truth?

She would forever be grateful He had.

Now when she looked around, the peace of her surroundings echoed inside her. She breathed in the scents—sage, wild roses, the heat lifting the smell of a thousand years from the soil.

Now wasn't she getting fanciful? She laughed out loud. At the sudden noise, a rabbit skittered from a nearby clump of grass and zigzagged a crazy path for several feet then crouched down, perfectly still. And as visible as a picture.

Queenie snorted.

"It's only a rabbit."

The horse whinnied and jerked her head. She

yanked away from the feeble bush and turned, kicked her heels once and headed down the hill.

Lucy bolted to her feet. "Stop."

Queenie didn't stop. She ran—the horse could run? She'd certainly hidden the fact until now.

Lucy raced after her but Queenie quickly outpaced her. "You stupid horse." Lucy staggered to a halt. So, now she walked.

Pausing, she took her bearings. The ranch lay to the east too shadowed for her to pick out in the distance.

Shadows?

She faced west. The sun hung low in the sky. How long had she been gone? A trickle of fear shivered through her. It would be dark before she could get back to the ranch. How would she find her way? She scanned the entire horizon. What if Indians found her?

God, help me.

She started to run, stumbled and caught herself before she fell facedown on the ground. Have to be careful. Don't want to break anything. Would Wade or Scout come looking for her?

She walked on, mindful of the rocks and holes she could trip on. It had been a long ride on Queenie's back.

It would be a much longer walk on her own two feet.

The shadows lengthened and sucked the light from

the ground. It would soon be too dark to see where she planted each foot.

Lord, keep me safe.

Lord, I put my confidence in You.

I trust Wade to be concerned about me when I don't return.

Scout, too?

She remembered how Scout had forgotten about her when he suspected Smitty was on the prowl. Perhaps she wasn't prepared to trust Scout that much just yet.

But surely Wade would find her. *Oh, please let him find me.*

Chapter Fifteen

Wade ducked into the house for a drink. "Lucy?" No answer. She must have gone down to the creek. For a moment he considered going after her and spending the rest of the afternoon in her sweet company. But Scout wanted to finish a wall today. And so did he.

He wiped his mouth and headed back to barn building.

Something bothered him as he crossed the yard. Something out of place but he couldn't quite put his finger on it.

But as he drove in spikes, the something tugged at his mind. "Isn't it about supper time?" he asked a little later. Lucy hadn't rung the triangle but he was more than ready to quit. "Let's head on in."

"Fine by me," Scout said as he put away the tools. "Roy, supper."

The boy jumped up from playing with the scraps of lumber and the three of them headed for the house.

Wade burst through first, the something he couldn't identify making him uneasy. He skidded to a halt. No food smells greeted them. Lucy did not stand at the stove tending a pot. The table was not set. "She isn't here."

Roy and Scout pushed past him.

"Lucy," Scout called. "Where are you, girl?"

"She's not here," Wade insisted. He didn't need to look to know it. He felt it in every pore.

Scout threw open her bedroom door. "Not here."

The something began to take shape. Wade spun around, raced for the corrals. Two Bit was grazing calmly nearby. Farther away the other horses fed. Except Queenie. "Where's your horse?" he asked Roy who, along with Scout, had followed him.

"She was here this morning."

"Likely nosing around to see if she can find some free oats." Wade vaulted the fence and ducked inside the barn. But no Queenie.

"Lucy must have gone out riding," Scout said. "'Spect she'll be back shortly."

"'Spect so." Wade agreed. But Lucy had never gone riding on her own before.

He couldn't shake the feeling something was wrong.

Scout and Roy returned to the house to await the meal but Wade stood in the middle of the yard, peering into the distance hoping to glimpse a twist of dust, a dark shuffling shape to indicate Queenie and a rider.

He strained for a sound. Nothing but the chirp of a nearby grasshopper and a snort from one of the horses.

Never had the prairies been so empty.

Wait. He heard a muffled thud and turned toward the sound. A horse. Queenie and Lucy? The animal drew closer and he recognized the lumbering gait. It was Queenie. He raced toward the horse. Within three steps he saw she carried no rider. "Lucy?" His voice brought a flurry of noise from the prairie as birds fluttered in protest of the sound.

Queenie jerked back at his roar and acted as if she might turn tail and run.

Wade forced himself to stop. To suck in air. Something had happened to Lucy and the only clue was this horse. He waited for the animal to edge closer and caught her. Sweated up. Had to have run a distance.

He snorted. A good hard run for Queenie was two hundred yards.

"My horse." Roy clattered off the step and ran toward them.

Wade gladly turned the animal over to him. "Better cool her down and brush her."

Scout waited on the step. "So, what's your take?"

"Either Lucy fell off, got tossed off or the stupid horse ran off and left her stranded."

"Either way she's out there somewhere and it will soon be dark."

Wade didn't need Scout to point out the obvious. "I'm going looking." He whistled for Two Bit and did a hundred yard dash to the corrals. The horse met him at the barn. In a few minutes Wade had the saddle on. Before he could swing up, Scout joined him.

"What direction are you going?"

Wade thought. "I can't imagine where she's gone." Or why? His heart thudded so hard it hurt his ribs. Sweat beaded his brow as he imagined Lucy hurt out in the vast prairie. "How will we find her?"

Scout gripped his shoulder. "We'll find her."

It registered that Scout offered to help.

"I haven't found my daughter only to lose her again."

Wade nodded. "And I haven't found the woman I want to spend the rest of my life with only to lose her."

Scout gave him a hard look as if realizing he'd found his daughter only to lose her to Wade if Wade got his way. Wade returned his look, resolve for resolve.

"I'll ride toward the big hill." Wade swung to his saddle.

"I'll head toward town."

"Roy?"

"I'll take him."

He accepted that Scout would always see Roy as a boy needing his attention. That was just fine with Wade. He was prepared to give Lucy all the attention she needed and wanted. "If you find her, fire off three shots. I'll do the same."

"Right."

"And leave a note in case she makes it back before we do."

Wade didn't wait for a reply. He galloped out of the yard. As he rode, he scanned the ground before him, squinted into the distance for anything that could be Lucy. Every few minutes, he paused to call her name and listened for a response. Listened for a moan. Or even a whisper.

Never had the prairies seemed so vast. So silent.

Darkness clutched at his shoulders. He shuddered. If Lucy were hurt, unable to call, he would never find her. He could ride past a few feet away and not know she was there.

Oh, God. You have answered so many of my prayers in the past. Too often I've looked at the answers for evidence of Your love. I know how foolish that is. I know you love me. I don't need any special signs and wonders. And today I am not asking for myself but for Lucy. Help me find her. Even if she never returns my love. Pain caused his arms to spasm at the thought. He shook his hands. Even if she never returned his love he wanted to see her safe.

Darkness deepened. He fought back despair. God would help him find her.

His plan had been to ride to the hill where he could see for miles but now he would see nothing. Still, it might be the best place to hear if she called. He kept Two Bit on a steady course toward the hill. He started to climb. Paused to call, "Lucy." His voice growing thick and strained with every passing hoofbeat.

A whisper came on the night air. Perhaps only a bird shuffling in protest to this unfamiliar noisy interruption.

It came again, stronger. More formed. About to move onward, he stopped. "Lucy?"

He turned his head trying to catch the sound. There. There it was. Definitely not a bird.

"Lucy, is that you? Keep calling."

He followed the sound until he made out the word, "Here."

His ribs tightened so hard he gasped. Lucy. Where was she? He called again, listened for her response.

"Here. Keep coming."

And then he could make out her shape against the gray sky. She stood upright. His breath whooshed out. At least she wasn't injured—he hoped. He dropped from his horse and picked his way across the rough ground, controlling his urge to fly to her side. "Are you hurt?"

"No. Just mad because Queenie ran off. Didn't know she had it in her."

He grinned at the angry regret in her voice. "She was all lathered up when she got home." He closed the distance between them and grabbed her shoulders. "You're sure you're fine?"

"Now that you're here, I am good. Really really good."

He pulled her into his arms and held her like fragile china. "You scared me some, I don't mind admitting."

"I don't mind at all that you do." Although her voice was muffled against his shirtfront, he detected a smile and let his hopes soar that she was pleased about more than being rescued. He'd ask her just as soon as he could be certain of speaking without his voice cracking.

He couldn't seem to let her go and noticed she made no effort to withdraw from his embrace.

"I was just a tiny bit scared that no one would come looking for me," she whispered.

His arms tightened even as his heart squeezed with painful realization that it would take her a long time to overcome her feelings of being overlooked. He pressed his cheek to her hair, reveling in the texture. As long as he lived, he hoped and prayed he could enjoy this privilege. "Lucy, I would have looked for you day and night until I found you."

She nodded against his chest. "I know."

Her confession tore away any residual doubt that she could ever trust him because of Scout. He grinned into the darkness. *Thank You, God.* "Scout is out looking for you, too. I better signal him." But it required he release her and get the rifle from the boot on the saddle. He couldn't make himself do so just yet.

"Are you sending him smoke signals I can't see?"

He chuckled. "I have to fire off three shots."

"Oh." She understood he must move but her arms slipped around his waist and he knew she couldn't bear the thought of letting go any more than he could. His heart practically flew from his chest. "Lucy gal, I don't think I'll let you out of my sight for a good long time." And if he had his way, not more than a few feet and a few minutes.

"Sounds like a promise."

"It is. It's my promise to love you and keep you and protect you all my life. If you'll let me."

She shifted to look into his face. In the darkness he could barely make out her features though he had no need for the light to know the color and shape and size of every one of them. "I should have let you know where I was going but I was…I guess mostly hurt and a little angry."

He searched his thoughts for a reason. Found none. "I don't understand."

"I overheard Scout saying he'd make you a

partner because you succeeded in getting me to come here."

"Yeah. Surprised me some." The man had never so much as suggested such a thing. "Shows just how much he appreciates having you come."

She sighed. "I didn't want the reason you brought me here to be so you'd get part of the ranch. I wanted…"

He held her within the circle of his arms, wanting to keep her there forever. Only closer. Right against his heart. "Lucy, what did you want?"

"I wanted there to be no selfish reason."

Ahh. He saw now. She thought he'd expected some reward for bringing her. "You're overlooking one small thing. I only brought you because you were trying to avoid Smitty."

She stiffened but still didn't pull out of his arms. "That worked out rather well for you, I'd say."

"I'd say so, too. I only wanted to repay Scout for his kindness. At least at first. But after I saw you in the dining room laughing and teasing and so full of life, I wanted you to come for my sake." Slowly, giving her lots of chance to resist, he pulled her closer until he breathed in her warm breath. "I hoped against hope that somehow, someday I would persuade you to come with me wherever I went."

"I think you might have succeeded."

Overflowing with love, he lowered his head, found her mouth and gave her the gentlest of kisses. When she responded by splaying her hands on his back, a gesture that sent sweet responses thrilling through him, he allowed himself a deeper, claiming kiss. Restraining his urge to kiss her for the rest of the night, he eased back. "I love you, Lucy Hall."

"I love you, Wade Miller."

"Now I better signal Scout." He pulled the rifle out and fired the three shots. "Let's get back to the house."

Lucy sat behind Wade, clinging to his back as they rode toward home. She pressed her face into the warmth of his shirt. Home. This was home. Wherever Wade was. His love had taught her where she belonged—with those who loved her and showed it as best they could. Someday she would tell him how her perceptions had changed while on his hilltop. For now, she wanted only to share her newfound way of looking at life with those who mattered most to her.

They arrived back at the house. Wade lifted her down and left Two Bit standing at the corrals. The fact that he showed more concern for her safe journey into the house than for his horse's care brought a smile of contentment to her face.

"Wait here while I light a lamp." He made her stand at the door until a golden glow filled the room, then he drew her close to the light. With fingers as gentle as the brush of cat fur he examined her cheeks, her chin, her forehead. "I want to make sure you're fine."

Smiling so hard her eyes felt glittery, she lifted her face and let him find out for himself just how fine she was. "I am better than fine. I am better than good. Life is full of sweet promise thanks to you."

"Me?" His eyes crinkled at the corners as he frowned. "What do you mean?"

It would take the rest of her life to tell him all the ways because she knew she could continually find more things to appreciate about him. "You brought me here. You showed me how constant love could be. And you—" Her voice caught. "You showed Scout and I how to start over."

He kissed her nose. "You would have figured it out without my help."

She wondered if they would. "Do you want to be a partner with him?"

He shrugged. "I haven't thought of it but I would like to settle down and I think it would be great if we could live close to Scout so you two could be a family. But none of that is important right now. Tell me you'll marry me and make me the happiest man in the world."

"I will marry you and I will be the happiest woman anywhere. And I will live with you wherever you want."

They kissed then.

The door burst open and Roy rushed in. He

skidded to a stop. "You're kissing." His voice rang with disgust.

Wade and Lucy laughed, their gazes holding each other, their eyes filled with secret joys.

Scout followed after Roy. "You're safe." He crossed the room and hugged Lucy. "Praise God." He looked slightly embarrassed as he released her.

It was the first hug she'd ever had from her father and she knew she would cherish it in a special place in her heart forever. However, she vowed it would not be the last time.

He shook Wade's hand, pumping it hard. "I hope you won't mind sharing her with me. We have a lot of years to catch up."

Wade caught Lucy's hand and pulled her close. "What do you think, Lucy?"

His smile filled her with sweet delight and courage. Then she turned to Scout. "I think I'd like that, Pa." The word came out slowly, hesitantly but she meant it wholly.

Scout's eyes filled with tears. He swiped them away.

Roy watched them, his eyes narrowed, his lips tight as he rocked back and forth. Lucy understood his concern. Knew he wondered if he had been forgotten. She held out a hand. "Come here, Roy."

He hesitated, wanting them all to know he didn't need them.

Lucy guessed the others knew as well as she

that he needed them and wanted them. "Come over here."

He shuffled forward until she could reach down and capture his hand. She pulled him to her side. "Anyone here object to Roy being part of this family?"

Wade and Scout spoke together. "Nope."

Wade opened his arms to pull Roy to Lucy's side. He wrapped his other arm around Scout's shoulders. Lucy pressed to Wade's side. "I'm not much for praying out loud," Wade said. "But this seems to be an occasion that calls for thanking God. So if none of you object…."

For answer, Scout and Roy bowed their heads.

Lucy held Wade's gaze just long enough to mouth the words, "I love you," before she, too, bowed.

"God, I thank You for bringing us all together and for answering so many of my prayers. I know You will continue to bless us and teach us. Above all I thank You for teaching us how to love. And I especially want to thank You for Lucy's love. Amen."

Lucy's heart filled with joy as she lifted her gaze to Wade and drank in his love.

Epilogue

Three months later, Lucy stood in the still-new church facing Lark's new preacher. She wore a pale gray gown that she knew brought out the gray in her eyes—though she needed nothing to help reveal the sparkle of happiness there. The past weeks had been a blur of joy. Wade, confident of her love, had surprised her with the many ways he found to show his love and appreciation. She knew in the passing years their love would grow sweeter and more dear.

At her side stood Wade. He looked extremely handsome in his black suit jacket. The look he gave her filled her with delight. Today they would become man and wife.

He hadn't wanted to wait but Pa had insisted he would build a smaller house for himself and Roy. "I will always think of this house as yours," he'd said to Lucy. With each passing day she grew more confident of her father's love and her years of feeling he didn't see her or want her began to heal.

Roy would be nurtured under Pa's care, with Lucy and Wade's love, as well.

The preacher began, "Dearly beloved, we are here to witness the joining of this man and this woman in the bonds of matrimony. A union designed by God for our mutual enjoyment."

Lucy blinked back tears of joy.

Thanks to God's faithfulness, she had learned how to trust and in response, she would soon enjoy the state of marriage.

A few minutes later, the preacher called for the ring. As Scout searched for it, Wade leaned close and whispered in her ear. "I will thank God every day of my life for your love."

She whispered back, "And I for yours."

He placed the ring on her finger then kissed her with his promise on his lips.

And then the preacher announced, "Mr. and Mrs. Miller."

Roy sighed loudly. "Now can we eat? I'm starved."

* * * * *

Dear Reader,

I love prairie ranches. The sky is so big. The view goes on forever. The colors vary from sharp blue to faded green. The view to some might appear flat and boring (We prairie folk have a saying, "Your dog can run away for a week before he's out of sight.") but if you pause and take a good look you see surprising details.

I think the prairies make a great setting for a romance. It's a place too big to be ignored. A landscape that sucks at your senses. A stillness that forces you to dig deep inside yourself. It's the perfect place for wounded characters to face their fears and confront their pasts.

I hope you enjoy this story of characters who find healing on a prairie ranch. I pray that if you have issues that need addressing, that reading how Lucy and Wade found healing will lead you toward God's love.

I love to hear from readers. If you want to tell me how this story worked for you, send me a message. You can find news about my books, me and a contact e-address on my Web site: www.lindaford.org.

Blessings,

Linda Ford

QUESTIONS FOR DISCUSSION

1. Lucy wanted no contact with her father. What had caused her to feel this way? Do you think she has reason to feel this way?

2. Lucy was happy with things the way they were. Should she have been more concerned about the past or the future?

3. Are there times when you need to give more consideration to the past or perhaps how your actions will impact the future?

4. In the story, Wade was motivated by the favor he owed Lucy's father. Did his motives change throughout the story? For the better or for worse?

5. It took a threat from an evil man to force Lucy to change her mind and agree to see her father. Do you think God had a hand in pushing her in this direction? Why or why not?

6. What challenges did the trio face in reaching the ranch? How do those challenges differ from what we might face today? How are they similar?

7. What had Wade found on the ranch that he'd longed for all his life? What longings are buried

in your heart and how could you satisfy them? Is God part of the answer? Share an example.

8. Wade felt unvalued as a child. Did he have reason for feeling this way? How do things from your childhood still affect you?

9. Do you feel Scout treated Lucy fairly after they were reunited? How did Lucy respond? Did you learn anything of value from their relationship?

10. The verse, "It is better to trust in the Lord than to put confidence in man," opened Lucy's eyes to the possibility of believing she could be loved. Are there situations in your life where this verse might apply?

11. Wade's faith has floundered. He's only beginning to learn to pray and trust God to answer. What can you learn from Wade's growing faith?

12. Roy found the family he wanted on the ranch. His willingness to belong seemed a contrast to Lucy's reluctance and fear of trust. Did you fear Roy would be hurt? Or do you think his openness made it easy for people to welcome him? Are there times in your life when you keep people back because of your fears?

13. Wade and Lucy found love. Lucy and Scout began a new father-daughter relationship. Roy found a home. But it's only the beginning of their lives together. Do you foresee happiness for them in the future? What can they do to ensure their continued happiness?

Love Inspired.
HISTORICAL

TITLES AVAILABLE NEXT MONTH
Available August 10, 2010

PATCHWORK BRIDE
Buttons & Bobbins
Jillian Hart

MISSION OF HOPE
Allie Pleiter

LIHCNM0710

REQUEST YOUR FREE BOOKS!

2 FREE INSPIRATIONAL NOVELS
PLUS 2
FREE
MYSTERY GIFTS

Love Inspired.
HISTORICAL
INSPIRATIONAL HISTORICAL ROMANCE

YES! Please send me 2 FREE Love Inspired® Historical novels and my 2 FREE mystery gifts (gifts are worth about $10). After receiving them, if I don't wish to receive any more books, I can return the shipping statement marked "cancel". If I don't cancel, I will receive 4 brand-new novels every other month and be billed just $4.24 per book in the U.S. or $4.74 per book in Canada. That's a saving of over 20% off the cover price. It's quite a bargain! Shipping and handling is just 50¢ per book.* I understand that accepting the 2 free books and gifts places me under no obligation to buy anything. I can always return a shipment and cancel at any time. Even if I never buy another book, the two free books and gifts are mine to keep forever.

102/302 IDN E7QD

Name	(PLEASE PRINT)	

Address		Apt. #

City	State/Prov.	Zip/Postal Code

Signature (if under 18, a parent or guardian must sign)

Mail to Steeple Hill Reader Service:
IN U.S.A.: P.O. Box 1867, Buffalo, NY 14240-1867
IN CANADA: P.O. Box 609, Fort Erie, Ontario L2A 5X3

Not valid for current subscribers to Love Inspired Historical books.

Want to try two free books from another series?
Call 1-800-873-8635 or visit www.morefreebooks.com.

* Terms and prices subject to change without notice. Prices do not include applicable taxes. Sales tax applicable in N.Y. Canadian residents will be charged applicable provincial taxes and GST. Offer not valid in Quebec. This offer is limited to one order per household. All orders subject to approval. Credit or debit balances in a customer's account(s) may be offset by any other outstanding balance owed by or to the customer. Please allow 4 to 6 weeks for delivery. Offer available while quantities last.

Your Privacy: Steeple Hill Books is committed to protecting your privacy. Our Privacy Policy is available online at www.SteepleHill.com or upon request from the Reader Service. From time to time we make our lists of customers available to reputable third parties who may have a product or service of interest to you. If you would prefer we not share your name and address, please check here. ☐

Help us get it right—We strive for accurate, respectful and relevant communications. To clarify or modify your communication preferences, visit us at www.ReaderService.com/consumerschoice.

LIH10R

HARLEQUIN®

A Romance

FOR EVERY MOOD™

Spotlight on
Heart & Home

Heartwarming romances
where love can happen
right when you least expect it.

See the next page to enjoy a sneak peek
from Harlequin® American Romance®,
a Heart and Home series.

*Five hunky Texas single fathers—five stories from
Cathy Gillen Thacker's* LONE STAR DADS *miniseries.
Here's an excerpt from the latest, THE MOMMY PROPOSAL
from Harlequin American Romance.*

"I hear you work miracles," Nate Hutchinson drawled.
Brooke Mitchell had just stepped into his lavishly appointed
office in downtown Fort Worth, Texas.

"Sometimes, I do." Brooke smiled and took the sexy
financier's hand in hers, shook it briefly.

"Good." Nate looked her straight in the eye. "Because
I'm in need of a home makeover—fast. The son of an old
friend is coming to live with me."

She was still tingling from the feel of his warm palm.
"Temporarily or permanently?"

"If all goes according to plan, I'll adopt Landry by
summer's end."

Brooke had heard the founder of Nate Hutchinson
Financial Services was eligible, wealthy and generous to a
fault. She hadn't known he was in the market for a family,
but she supposed she shouldn't be surprised. But Brooke
had figured a man as successful and handsome as Nate
would want one the old-fashioned way. *Not that this was
any of her business...*

"So what's the child like?" she asked crisply, trying not
to think how the marine-blue of Nate's dress shirt deepened
the hue of his eyes.

"I don't know." Nate took a seat behind his massive
antique mahogany desk. He relaxed against the smooth
leather of the chair. "I've never met him."

"Yet you've invited this kid to live with you permanently?"

"It's complicated. But I'm sure it's going to be fine."

Obviously Nate Hutchinson knew as little about teenage

boys as he did about decorating. But that wasn't her problem. Finding a way to do the assignment without getting the least bit emotionally involved was.

Find out how a young boy brings Nate and Brooke together in THE MOMMY PROPOSAL, coming August 2010 from Harlequin American Romance.

Love Inspired.
HISTORICAL
INSPIRATIONAL HISTORICAL ROMANCE

Bestselling author

JILLIAN HART

**brings readers
a new heartwarming story in**

Patchwork Bride

Meredith Worthington is returning to
Angel Falls, Montana, to follow her dream
of becoming a teacher. And perhaps get to know
Shane Connelly, the intriguing new wrangler on
her father's ranch. Shane can't resist her charm
even though she reminds him of everything he'd like
to forget. But will love have time to blossom before
she discovers the secret he's been hiding all along?

*Available in August
wherever books are sold.*

**Steeple
Hill®**

LIH82841